A drop of wild honey still glistened on her lips.

Nobody was more surprised than he when he leaned in.

He barely brushed his lips across hers, but he felt the impact all the way to his toes.

For a moment so brief that he might have imagined it, she went with the flow. Then she was pushing against him. He pulled away, searching her stunned face, trying to gather his scattered thoughts.

And with the symbolic distance between them, whatever craziness had possessed him disappeared. He didn't know where it had come from, but he did know one thing for sure: under no circumstances would he ever touch this woman again. She was nothing but trouble.

"We shouldn't be doing this. You are—" She paused. "I am—" She made a soft noise of frustration. "We can't do this again."

His gaze strayed to those ruby lips that were pressed into a severe, angry line. Then, instead of agreeing, he flashed the woman his most wicked grin and said, "I think we're definitely going to do this again."

DANA
MARTON

STRANDED WITH THE PRINCE

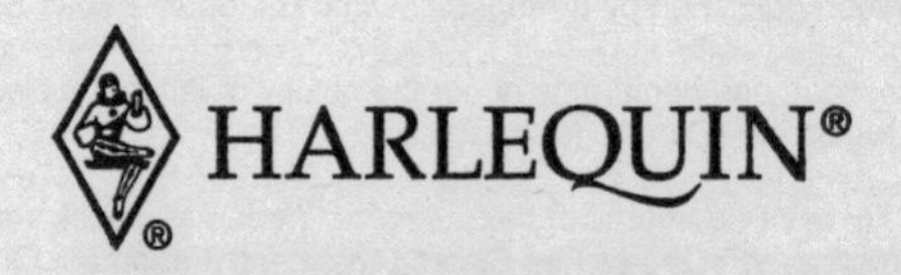

TORONTO • NEW YORK • LONDON
AMSTERDAM • PARIS • SYDNEY • HAMBURG
STOCKHOLM • ATHENS • TOKYO • MILAN • MADRID
PRAGUE • WARSAW • BUDAPEST • AUCKLAND

With many thanks to Allison Lyons

ISBN-13: 978-0-373-69473-0

STRANDED WITH THE PRINCE

This edition published by arrangement with Harlequin Books S.A.

For questions and comments about the quality of this book please contact us at Customer_eCare@Harlequin.ca.

www.eHarlequin.com

Printed in U.S.A.

ABOUT THE AUTHOR

Dana Marton is the author of more than a dozen fast-paced, action-adventure romantic suspense novels and a winner of the Daphne du Maurier Award of Excellence. She loves writing books of international intrigue, filled with dangerous plots that try her tough-as-nails heroes and the special women they fall in love with. Her books have been published in seven languages in eleven countries around the world. When not writing or reading, she loves to browse antiques shops and enjoys working in her sizable flower garden where she searches for "bad" bugs with the skills of a superspy and vanquishes them with the agility of a commando soldier. Every day in her garden is a thriller. To find more information on her books, please visit www.danamarton.com. She loves to hear from her readers and can be reached via e-mail at DanaMarton@DanaMarton.com.

Books by Dana Marton

HARLEQUIN INTRIGUE

806—SHADOW SOLDIER
821—SECRET SOLDIER
859—THE SHEIK'S SAFETY
875—CAMOUFLAGE HEART
902—ROGUE SOLDIER
917—PROTECTIVE MEASURES
933—BRIDAL OP
962—UNDERCOVER SHEIK
985—SECRET CONTRACT*
991—IRONCLAD COVER*
1007—MY BODYGUARD*
1013—INTIMATE DETAILS*
1039—SHEIK SEDUCTION
1055—72 HOURS
1085—SHEIK PROTECTOR
1105—TALL, DARK AND LETHAL
1121—DESERT ICE DADDY
1136—SAVED BY THE MONARCH†
1142—ROYAL PROTOCOL†
1179—THE SOCIALITE AND THE BODYGUARD
1206—STRANDED WITH THE PRINCE†

*Mission: Redemption
†Defending the Crown

CAST OF CHARACTERS

Lazlo Kerkay—The "rebel prince" is a successful entrepreneur and a ladies' man. But he hasn't seen trouble until he meets a determined matchmaker from the U.S. who is set on ending his freedom.

Milda Milas—The last in a long line of matchmakers, Milda is brought in from New York by the queen to help tame the wildest of the princes. Finding a match for Lazlo turns into the most difficult task she's ever attempted.

Roberto—The leader of a small group of criminals from Bogotá. He is in Europe to penetrate the European drug market and to gain revenge for his brother's death.

The Freedom Council—A secret group of prominent businessmen whose sole purpose is to destroy the royal family and break the country into small republics that they could each rule individually.

Arpad Kerkay—The crown prince is a colonel in the air force. Since the queen is ill, soon he will inherit the crown.

Miklos Kerkay—Second to the throne. He is an army major and a happily married man.

Janos Kerkay—Third in line to the throne. He is an economist and a superb yachtsman who also regularly wins golf championships.

Istvan Kerkay—The fourth prince in line to the throne is a cultural anthropologist who is obsessed with preserving the past of his country.

Benedek Kerkay—Lazlo's twin. The youngest prince has two passions: architecture and his wife, Rayne Williams, the opera singing sensation.

Chapter One

Sagro Prison island, Italy

Boots slapped on the concrete floor, keeping a regular rhythm. The night security lights were on, enough to see the guard who was texting on his phone as he strode out of sight, a sly grin on his pockmarked face. A minute went by, then another. The steel door opened then closed at the end of the cell block.

The 2:00 a.m. check was complete. Nobody would be by again until morning.

Roberto, fully dressed, slid out of bed, making no more noise than his shadow as it moved across the floor. He laid his pillow lengthwise on the bare mattress then draped the bed with his blanket, creating a bulky form.

His sheets had been ripped, twisted into rope and wrapped around his waist before he'd gone to bed. Now he bent and squatted one more time to make sure the cumbersome arrangement wouldn't limit his movement. He adjusted a tight strip under his left armpit before he stole to the door and pressed the top part of the lock hard.

Click. The sound was so soft even he barely heard it.

José had fixed the locks. The oldest of the team, José had been a locksmith before a drive-by took out his family in the godforsaken backstreets of Bogotá. With nothing to live for, he'd signed up for the rival gang. José understood revenge.

So did Roberto. It pushed him forward as he stole down the hallway, moving fast in a crouch. He listened to the snoring of the other inmates. A bed creaked now and then as someone turned over in his sleep. He listened for any indication that someone noticed him, not trusting—despite substantial bribes and dire threats—that they wouldn't betray him and sound the alarm.

José was waiting for him at the water block, along with Marco, the third member of the team.

"Any trouble?" Roberto kept his voice to a low whisper.

Marco shook his head. He was young and sullen, still not over the fact that they'd been imprisoned. That here, on the other side of the ocean, the boss couldn't protect them. He was ready to go, but didn't think it fair that they had to orchestrate the escape themselves. He'd griped and whined through the preparations. Which better stop right now, right here. Roberto flashed him a sharp look that warned him to be on his best behavior.

The young thugs coming out of the slums these days

were too hotheaded, only after the glory, and rarely willing to put enough effort into a job to get it done right. They wanted the fastest car and the biggest gun, wanted to build reputations overnight, which led to too much senseless killing.

"All's according to plan," José was saying.

Exactly what Roberto wanted to hear. His sticker, a spoon handle sharpened into a knife, waited stashed inside a showerhead. He retrieved the makeshift tool then went to work on removing a wall panel.

A hundred years ago, Sagro Prison had been the hunting castle of some Italian king. When they'd rebuilt it into a prison in the fifties, they changed just about everything. Security had been upgraded several times since, but the prison's waste and sewer system still connected to the old castle's cistern.

All Roberto and his men had had to do over the endless months that they'd been locked up here was dig through the wall. The cistern's ducts, carved from stone, were plenty wide to accommodate a man.

José squeezed in first, then Marco, Roberto going last, pulling the wall panel into place behind him. By morning they'd be free men. His to-do list was simple: get food, finish the boss's business in Trieste, then get the hell out of Italy.

But he wouldn't go back to Bogotá, not straightaway. He had personal business in the area which he meant to see handled. He was going to Valtria, the small kingdom to the north, to gain retribution for his brother's death.

An eye for an eye, a life for a life. He might have been too old-school to condone all the senseless killing the new gangs did these days, but revenge was part of a man's honor. And he did believe in that. He certainly did.

Island of Morka, Nature Preserve, Valtria

SHE WAS THE SCOURGE of his life, a relentless thorn under his royal skin. Prince Lazlo of Valtria watched Milda Milas bear down on him and knew what it felt like to be hunted.

A professional matchmaker from New York. He loved his mother as much as all his brothers did, but the Queen had gone too far this time. One of her ladies-in-waiting had a cousin in New York who'd been Milda's client. Apparently, a recommendation had been made. He didn't like the idea of his mother discussing his personal life with her ladies-in-waiting. Shouldn't they have been talking about the royal gardens or copying antique tapestries and the like when they retired to the Queen's private quarters?

Despite the calming, balmy breeze that streamed from the endless azure water, Lazlo's sense of peace was fast disappearing. He'd been looking forward to spending the day away from the palace, away from Milda's harping. He should have known she wouldn't let a perfectly good day go by without doing her best to ruin it. A dull throb started up in the knee he'd once injured in a crash. Maybe his subconscious was beginning to associate her with pain.

"And there I was, thinking I could hide from you here," he said when she reached him.

He liked the island of Morka, fifty miles off the Italian coast, an inhabited chunk of land in the Mediterranean Sea, owned by the Valtrian royal family and set up as a nature preserve. With its wild olive and orange groves, the place was a veritable paradise—but for Milda Milas's unfortunate presence.

"Your Highness." She stopped in front of him with that ra-ra-hurra look that hardly left her face whenever she dealt with him. She seemed to think that if she smiled wide enough and pretended that what she was doing to him was normal—wonderful, even—somehow he could be tricked into agreeing with her.

"I don't know how you got here. Never mind that." He reconsidered and cut to the point. "You should leave," he told her firmly. "I'm not playing your games today. I've made other plans."

Since the top of her head only came up to his shoulders, she usually rose to the tips of her toes when she wanted to browbeat him into yet another one of her crazy plans. She was stretching up so hard at the moment that she looked like a ballet dancer. The wind whipped her long, reddish-brown hair around her slim face. Her eyes, the exact dusky blue of his first race car, narrowed as she dropped the smile, recognizing smartly that it wasn't going to work today.

"You should face your responsibilities, Your

Highness. Don't you think all this endless evasion is childish?"

She had his gander up in thirty seconds flat. A new record. She knew she was annoying him, but she didn't care. She had the Queen's protection. She'd been given free reign, God help him.

"I'm childish?" He drew up an eyebrow slowly, regally, and regarded her with a chilly expression he'd learned early on in life from his mother. "You torture me for money. What does that make you?"

She dropped back on her heels and stuck her chin out, her eyes and lips narrowing. "To be honest, I'd torture you for free. If that makes you feel better."

He was taken aback for a moment. He was used to more respect as a prince. Although not from her, admittedly.

"You know what I think?" she asked with a smirk, losing the last of her polite veneer.

He allowed a subtle sneer. "A better question is, mademoiselle, do I care?"

"I think you're afraid that you couldn't hold an intelligent woman's attention over the long term. That's why you engage only in nightlong, scandalous affairs with those twits." Her tone turned to lecturing. "Your conduct is embarrassing the monarchy and the Queen. You were caught on tape in a compromising situation, for love's sake." She rolled her dusky blue eyes in a way that told him exactly what she thought of that.

Not that until now he'd been forced to guess. She

had expressed her opinion a number of times since the unfortunate incident.

He tried to put this latest scandal out of his mind. No chance of that with her around. *She* was going to lecture him on his duties as a prince? His blood pressure inched up. He drew a long, slow breath.

"You know what I think?" he asked, and kept going, without giving her a chance to pipe up. "I think American kamikaze nuptial consultants should stay in their own country."

He was pleased with himself for resisting the urge to raise his voice. He was not going to lose control because of her. He was a prince. He was certainly up to the challenge of ignoring a troublesome matchmaker. "Where are my brothers?"

He was supposed to be on the island with them, and *only* them, on a day hike. Miklos's idea. Since the failed rebel attacks of the past two years, the six royal brothers hardly got to spend time together anymore. If he didn't like Miklos's and Benedek's wives so much, he would have blamed it on them, but Princess Judi and Princess Rayne were too lovely to fault for anything. He couldn't truly blame his brothers for not wanting to leave home, even if he never understood what had possessed them to rush into marriage.

Single life suited him just fine. Being a prince, he already had more expectations and regulations, more rules governing his every move than he cared to think about. Marriage would have been just another prison.

Which Milda refused to understand.

"Your brothers aren't coming." Her slim fingers worried the colorful bead bracelet on her left wrist.

Why couldn't they just call, instead of sending a message with her, of all people, when— Lazlo froze, a terrible premonition holding him speechless for a moment before he could ask, "This is another one of your traps, isn't it?"

So help him God—

"You'll be going hiking with the Lady Lidia, the Lady Szilvia and the Lady Adel." Her "this will be fun, you'll see" smile returned.

He swore in a way that should have been beneath him as a prince. "My brothers helped you set me up?" A new low. Incomprehensible, really. The sense of betrayal was overwhelming.

And her guilty look confirmed everything.

His brothers probably thought it was a grand joke. "I'm going to murder them," he muttered.

History was full of princes who killed their own brothers to get closer to the throne. He didn't care about the throne. But he might be driven to murder by Milda Milas yet. Except, then centuries from now historians would speculate that maybe he'd been secretly in love with her, and the act had been motivated by jealousy or some such nonsense. That would be intolerable. She was already messing up his life; he wasn't going to let her sully his legacy.

"How dare you?" He stepped toward her, ready to take her to task, but caught sight of a sizable pile of duffel bags farther up the beach. He'd thought them a pile of rocks earlier, with the sun in his eyes, but now that a small cloud blocked some of the brilliant rays, he could see that he'd been mistaken. "What is that?"

They couldn't have needed all that equipment for one day. His own guards were in the process of unloading his speedboat, removing the two boxes that contained the food and drink he and his brothers would have needed until they returned to the palace this evening.

"A two-week hike?" she squeaked, cleared her throat, went back up on her tiptoes then said again, in a deeper tone of self-confidence she must have practiced in the mirror, "A two-week hike with the ladies." Her damned smile was in full bloom.

He glanced around but didn't see any desperate women ready to drag him to the altar. Excellent. He had plenty of time to run for the boat. "Have you lost your mind?"

She drew her slim shoulders up, looking like some sort of exotic bird taking up defensive position. Or getting ready to attack. He had the uncomfortable feeling that he was about to be pecked to death.

"The ladies went to see the Painted Rocks. They should be back shortly. You need to spend time with intelligent, self-sufficient women, and stay away from your empty-headed beauties for a few days," she stated.

So she admitted that the three ladies in question weren't beauties. Not that he could bring that up without proving himself to be shallow—of which she accused him endlessly.

The impatient growl that escaped him didn't seem to alarm her in the least. "Once you calm down, Your Highness, you'll see this was a good idea." She didn't back away. She never backed down from him, one of her many annoying qualities. "By tonight, I promise you'll feel a lot better about all this."

The only thing that would have made him feel better would have been tossing her into the sea. Sadly, being a prince, he'd been raised better than to threaten bodily harm to a woman. Not even a woman who was dead set on ruining his life.

She wasn't going to quit until she saw him married. She was the type to see that the job got done. No matter what. In anyone else, he could have appreciated the drive. He could appreciate little in her. They'd been doing battle for months now.

A wave of weariness hit him. "Why are you doing this to me?"

Her gaze never wavered. "For one, as you pointed out, I get paid for it."

"I could pay you more to go away."

"I would never break my contract. You should be grateful. I'm here to help you. The Queen gave you six months to announce that you've chosen a bride. She wants to see you settled down. You must end the scandals."

"I still have another month." In fact, he'd been counting on that last month of freedom rather desperately.

"Exactly."

"Two weeks on this blasted island would waste half.

Absolutely not. When that boat leaves in a few minutes, I'm leaving with it."

"And the ladies? Common courtesy—"

"If you want to stay with the ladies, be my guest. Have a pajama party." He ignored the intriguing picture that flashed into his mind and focused on her clenched jaw instead.

But the next moment she was forcing a smile again. He hated how cheerful she always was while she tortured him.

"Two weeks in this beautiful place is exactly what you need." She sounded like she actually believed it. "By the time we come back for you, you will have made your choice. The Queen and the country will be happy."

"Dare I ask, what about me?"

"Try to give these women a chance. Maybe you'll fall in love with one of them." Her eyes brightened at the mention of the L word.

"In two weeks?" Was she for real? Sadly, she was. She had an unshakable, deep-seated belief in romance that annoyed the hell out of him. He gave her his most discouraging expression, the one he normally reserved for ambushing paparazzi.

But her eyebrows stayed up, the corners of her lips tugged into that fake encouraging smile, her gaze steady on him. "Stranger things have happened."

A *lot* of strange things had happened to him lately, his mother hiring the pushiest woman in the world to force him to wed being one of them. But the chances of him falling in love were slim to none. For that to happen, he would have to believe in love to begin with.

There was no point in further bickering with her. They were too different. They'd never understand each other. He glanced at the boat, ready to go, and realized that the two guards had disappeared, leaving the boxes of food on the bluff above the tide line. "Where did Ben and Vince go?"

She worried her bead bracelet again for a brief, unguarded moment before she responded. "They'll guard the island's perimeter. They'll be in radio contact with each other, but not with you. I can't risk you bullying them with some fake emergency into coming to pick you up."

The woman boggled his mind. She was beyond all belief. "Good plan." He couldn't help a sneer. "And what would have happened if there'd *been* an emergency?"

"I'm not at liberty to say," she said, apparently still thinking that she could make him stay.

He glanced toward his jacket, draped over the side of the boat, his cell phone in the pocket. He needed to pay closer attention to her. She wasn't to be underestimated. With some luck, she *could* have stranded him. The thought was disturbing.

He needed to make her see reason and quit this sordid business. "You really expected me to spend two weeks in the bush with a bunch of wilting lilies? I'm a racer, not a camper. And I bet your ladies haven't seen more nature than what can be found at the palace gardens. What, exactly, did you think we would be doing out here?"

She put that pert nose of hers into the air and flashed him a smug look. "Lady Lidia is an herbalist, Lady Szilvia is a survival specialist and Lady Adel is a doctor at your favorite ski resort."

He sure didn't remember her. Which must have meant she wasn't a looker. Then again, he preferred to sustain his injuries at the racetrack, so maybe he hadn't been visited by the resort's doctor in the past.

"I'm to attend a race tomorrow evening." It was to be the first time one of his cars was running with a modified engine, a major invention he needed to see in action. He needed to make manufacturing decisions based on tomorrow's race. She was interfering with his business.

"Prince Lazlo—"

"Enough." He was out of patience with her and her meddling. She'd been relentlessly after him for the past five months, since the Queen and Chancellor Egon had sicced her on him. "So you decided to parade the country cows." He practically growled the words. "You need to understand, Milda, that I'm not some prize bull you can lead into the pasture for breeding."

"Prince Laz—"

"No." He raised a hand, palm out. "I don't care what these women want from me—title, money or their children in the line of succession. They need to find another way of getting it. So you collected a homely bunch of ambitious—" he swallowed the word that a prince wouldn't utter "—ladies. Read my lips. I don't want any of them." He pushed by her to stride toward the boat.

"Prince Lazlo!"

"Goodbye, Milda."

But something in her voice as she called his name again stopped him. He turned to give her a piece of his mind, in case she still harbored some doubts regarding how he felt about the evil job she'd been hired to do.

And he saw the three ladies.

They had come out of the wild olive grove. From the look on their faces, they'd been standing within hearing range when he'd made that country cow comment. *Blast it,* he thought.

By God, he was tired of this. He liked the chase between the sexes, another sport to him. But, call him old-fashioned, he liked to be the one to do the chasing. He inclined his head, his jaw so tight he could barely push out the single word. "Ladies."

They looked vaguely familiar—and were pretty, to be fair—but he couldn't place them. No big surprise there. He'd run into a lot of women over the years.

"Your Highness." They curtsied, but if looks could kill…

Which was surprising. The women he regularly saw at court were more of the simpering kind—lots of eyelash batting and that sort of thing. He hated simpering. But maybe these three were different. Maybe Milda had done her homework.

He still didn't care. He wasn't going to be forced into marriage.

What a crazy, absolutely insane idea this has been—him on a deserted island with three proper young ladies. Ridiculous, really. For two weeks!

He gave them an apologetic smile he had to force. They'd been inconvenienced as much as he had. "I'm sorry you've been misled. Why don't you wait in the boat? I'll take you back to the mainland in a minute."

The boat could only seat four. Which meant Milda and the two bodyguards would have to wait until someone returned for them. Now there was a happy thought. With some luck, the pickup would take a long time. For a moment, he even toyed with the thought of not sending his boat back. Two weeks of freedom without her hounding him... The idea held considerable merit.

"See what you've done?" he asked, once the ladies were out of earshot, as they marched toward the boat. Obedient they were, he couldn't help noticing. After dealing with Milda for the past five challenging months, he was beginning to appreciate obedience more and more in a woman. "You managed to further damage my reputation. You should quit and go home to New York. You're a PR liability."

No evidence of her infamous smile now. Her face was turning red. Her delicate nostrils flared. He wouldn't have been surprised to see smoke coming out of her dainty ears.

"I damaged your reputation?" She put her hands on her slim hips. The movement stretched her shirt over her breasts. They were one of her very best features, made the endless hours she spent lecturing him bearable. "*I* damaged your reputation?" She was sputtering.

"You can think of ways to make it up to me while you wait for someone to come for you." He smirked as he stepped away from her, ready to saunter across the beach.

"I'm fighting for my business," she warned him. "My livelihood and my heritage. I will *not* give up. I will not give in."

"And I'm fighting for my freedom. Something I most cherish," he told her…and heard the motor start.

He spun around in time to see the boat pull away, steered by Lady Adel.

"Wait!" Sand flew up around him as he broke into a sprint. His busted knee slowed him. And the boat was too far, pulling away rapidly.

They couldn't leave him, dammit. Not here, not with Milda. "Wait!" He dashed into the surf after them to no avail. But he refused to give up. He swam like he never swam before. Like his life depended on it.

One of the ladies gave him a smug little wave.

The distance between them was growing.

And growing.

His lungs burned from the effort he put into propelling his body through the water. Then he stopped completely, at last accepting the unacceptable. He swore an unprincely streak and let himself sink for a moment, let the waves wash over his head before he pushed up to the surface again. He treaded water for another few seconds, too stunned to think. Then, as outrage took over, he turned to swim for the shore.

He strode back onto dry land, fuming and dripping. "You!" He bore down on the woman of his nightmares. "Get on your cell phone and get another boat out here."

Her stricken look stopped him. They were practically nose to nose anyway, only inches separating them from each other. Her big blue eyes went impossibly wide. She smelled like spring, the perfume the Queen's own *parfumerie* had created for her, a scent that lately haunted him, even in his sleep.

"I want another boat. Pronto. As in yesterday." He barked the words at her.

She was very quiet all of a sudden.

He didn't have the patience for this. "Speak."

"My organizer fell into the water on the way here with the ladies." She winced. "I'm a bad swimmer. I always get nervous around water. I should have—"

"I don't care about your organizer." The damn thing was her ever-present companion. Her nefarious plans for his life were no doubt in it. He'd been so disconcerted by her sudden appearance on the island that he hadn't even noticed it was missing. "Good riddance."

"My cell phone was tucked in the front."

He walked away from her before he said something he regretted. But called back, after a moment, "Will the guards be checking on us?"

"No." Her voice was small. A first. "They're supposed to avoid contact at all costs. They're to stay out of sight at all times. They won't be following you or anything. We, um, wanted to give you and the ladies privacy. The guards are only here to prevent the paparazzi from getting on the island if they get wind of your trip. For all intents and purposes, we're alone on an uninhabited island. That's the feel I was going for to foster a certain sense of..."

He glared, daring her to say the word "romance." That and true love were her favorite things. He'd tried to tell her in vain that there came a time when a grown woman should stop believing in fairy tales.

She closed her mouth without finishing the sentence, but she didn't fool him. She was hopeless. He turned from her again, to survey the shore. There had to be a way off.... He thought of something suddenly. She was very methodical about ruining his life. She was definitely the type to plan for contingencies.

He turned back to her. "What was the emergency plan? If I broke an arm, how would I have called for help?" He was a royal person. There was always a backup plan for unforeseen contingencies.

She was studying her feet, her sandals half sunk into the soft sand. "The Lady Adel had an emergency radio in her medical bag," she muttered.

"The red bag on her shoulder?" He distinctly remembered the bag. It was the one the doctor walked to the boat with.

Milda nodded weakly. "They'll send someone back for us as soon as they land." She looked after them, biting her bottom lip. The women and his speedboat were a dot over endless blue waves. "We'll be back at the palace before nightfall, I'm sure."

He wouldn't bet on it. "So basically, we could be stranded here for two whole weeks."

She still avoided his gaze. "I wanted to give you sufficient time to get comfortable with each other. I wanted to give the ladies enough time for their true colors to start showing. I only meant the best for you. For everybody."

A minute or so passed in uncomfortable silence, as they both contemplated the absurdity of the situation.

Then she finally looked him in the eye. "Have you camped before?"

He shook his head. "You?"

Her face looked pinched. "I have a demanding business that I run all by myself. I don't usually leave the city."

ROBERTO PUT ONE HAND above the other as he climbed the guard tower soundlessly. Below him, Sagro Prison was clouded in darkness, the island quiet. He gripped his sole weapon, the sharpened handle of a spoon, between his teeth. When he reached the top, he vaulted over and cut the guard's throat before the man could raise the alarm.

Had to be done.

There was no way around it. He lowered the body to the wooden boards, wiped the warm blood off his fingers and took the rifle, waited.

No siren sounded. He hadn't been detected. The

small Italian prison island was well guarded, but it was no high-security facility.

He lowered himself to the ground where José and Marco crouched in the shadows. He was the boss of the small team, though they were all hired hands, working for a new Colombian drug lord who was trying to break into the European market via Italy, among other places. Except that they'd been caught on this trip.

But he wouldn't rot in a dank cell, he thought as they crawled their way to the fence where the hole they'd painstakingly prepared and covered awaited. He wouldn't end up like his brother, Miguel, trapped in a Valtrian prison, then knifed by some local hotshot, dead two weeks before his release.

The drug lord they both worked for was trying to wiggle his way into the European market at multiple points of entry. Roberto had a cousin with a small team in Romania. He wondered how the bastard was faring. Hopefully better than this.

He was the first to reach the unfinished tunnel and head into the darkness. What little they'd left for tonight could be done in an hour. He dug with the flat rock they'd used to get this far, sweated, swore, but never stopped working. When at long last he'd reached the opening, only just clearing the fence, he tossed the stone aside then brushed the dirt from his eyes.

"Hurry," he said, speaking for the first time. This far out, nobody should be able to hear them.

He came up into a crouch, suddenly dizzy from hunger. All three of them were starving. Over the past few weeks, they'd had to bribe too many inmates with food to get what they needed for the escape. They could have just as easily beaten the bastards into obedience, but fights drew the guards' attention, and their small team needed to fly below the radar. They had to remain invisible. Then and now.

"Keep low to the ground," he said as they crossed the narrow slice of flat plateau. Then they unraveled their makeshift ropes, tied them together and lowered themselves down the rock face.

Roberto reached the beach first. When they were all down, they gathered as much driftwood as they could find, then they used the ropes to tie a raft together. Marco was the fastest with the knots, the son of a fisherman, pulling his weight for the first time. They swam out beyond the breakers before climbing on, then paddled with their shoes as best they could—which wasn't easy at all, as the waves were getting angry.

Real paddles would have helped, but they'd had no place to steal them from and no time to make them. Using their shoes required too much effort for too little result. The three were weak and exhausted, but they would work until their last breath.

They'd all sworn not to go back behind bars. They would either escape today or die trying.

"Get your ass moving." Roberto snarled at Marco when he slowed. The other apparently thought that having worked on the raft, he was now entitled to a break.

José shook his head and spit into the waves.

Marco got back to the paddling sullenly.

More trouble than he was worth. But they weren't out of danger yet. Roberto still needed him.

They needed to take the current to the mainland, land in an out-of-the-way spot and disappear deep into the country by morning, when their breakout would be discovered and law enforcement would start their coastal search.

But a storm was coming in and the waves didn't cooperate. The current seemed to be changing, taking them in another direction entirely.

Chapter Two

In hindsight, they shouldn't have wasted so much of the daylight on fighting.

Milda wrestled with the tent she'd dragged into the olive grove. She could see Prince Lazlo's outline a few hundred yards from her. She hadn't gone too far—was kind of scared of the darkness of the grove, the trees throwing shadows in the moonlight. The island was a nature preserve. Which meant wild animals for sure. She didn't want to think about that.

"I don't think that's how it goes," the prince called across the distance that separated them. He hadn't bothered bringing the second tent up from the beach.

"I got it," she answered over her shoulder. *Don't come over. Please, don't come over.*

If he helped her set up her tent, he would probably expect to sleep in it. With her. She couldn't handle that.

She glanced toward him. He rested—probably thinking dark, murderous thoughts about her—sitting up, his back against a tree, his shoulders outlined in the dim light. His body was lithe and powerful. He wasn't her favorite person in the world, but even she had to admit that he was incredibly handsome, with that debonair, devil-may-care attitude.

And beyond his good looks, he was intelligent as well. And a prince. At first, she'd been foolish enough to think that marrying him off would be easy. He'd certainly taught her better since.

She couldn't pin the man down, not for a second. Like seawater through a fishnet, he ran through her fingers over and over again. He could have made it all work. He had incredible focus when he chose. He owned one of the best speed car factories in Europe, built it himself from nothing but a dream. When he wanted something, he applied himself to the task until he achieved his goal. He could have made her job easy. Instead, he was doing the opposite. He didn't want anything to do with the Queen's plans, so he resisted Milda at every step.

Like the damn tent was doing at the moment.

She was going to figure this out. She gathered her last reserves and fitted the poles together at last. And felt triumphant.

Until she tried to get the structure in through the tent's door. She struggled for at least five minutes before she figured out it wasn't going to work this way. The poles were probably supposed to be snapped into place *inside* the tent. She stifled a groan and took it all apart.

"Need help?"

"Almost done. I'll be ready in a minute." She looked up to make sure he wasn't coming over.

But he was still sitting by the tree, his aristocratic profile outlined by the last of the light—a strong chin, straight nose and lips that looked as if they were carved from granite. Aside from the occasional debauchery—or even *with* that—he could have been one of those heroes of ancient Rome. She could definitely see him at the chariot races. She'd seen him at a modern racetrack, behind the wheel.

He was mesmerizing, had charisma in spades. No wonder women fell at his feet left and right. He certainly spent more time with them than pondering the duties of royalty. To the point that the media had taken to calling him The Rebel Prince. She filled her lungs with the salty sea air and turned away from him, giving the impertinent tent her full attention once again.

"I can't believe the women didn't send the boat back," she said after another five minutes of struggle.

"You know, the blonde looked familiar. I think I might have dated her in the past."

"You dated all three of them. With time being so tight, I wanted to go for certainty. A shortcut, you know? If you were attracted to them once, you could be attracted to them again."

Silence was the only answer.

"Right?" she asked, then immediately hated that she was second-guessing herself because of him. He was terrible for her self-confidence.

"'Heaven has no rage like love to hatred turned, nor

hell a fury like a woman scorned.'" He quoted William Congreve. "Better settle in for the full two weeks."

"They couldn't have been that mad at you. They agreed to another try."

"Could be they planned to kill me in the wilderness," he remarked dryly.

"What on earth have you done to them? No, never mind." The fact that he didn't even remember that he'd dated them gave her a clue. Plus his tirade on the beach that the ladies had overheard. She'd never dated him, and even she was about ready to strangle him and leave him in the wilderness for the vultures or whatever.

So maybe the ladies were somewhat justified in their fury. But leaving *her* stranded here with the prince was completely uncalled for. What harm had *she* done to anyone? She was doing the best she could, with everyone's best interests at heart. She was beginning to feel decidedly underappreciated. The least of her problems, all considered, when her whole world was threatening to come right down around her ears.

She was the last link in a long line of matchmakers. And the business hadn't been doing well for the past couple of years. If she failed, the family tradition would end with her. Her grandmother was probably rolling in her grave.

Poles miraculously snapping into place and holding the tent up from the inside at last distracted her from any further thoughts on what a disappointment she was turning out to be, compared to her more talented ancestors. The tent was standing. So there. That was something. She pulled herself straight proudly, grinning into the darkness. But then she tripped over the blanket she'd already tossed into the tent, not wanting it to get dirty or bugs to crawl inside, and fell with her full weight against one of the poles and the whole thing came apart all over again.

She could have howled with frustration. She didn't. She'd be damned if she'd lose control within hearing distance of the prince.

"Everything okay in there?" His voice dripped with mockery.

She climbed out on her hands and knees, the definition of undignified, stood and brushed herself off. "I decided to take it down. The air is too stifling in there."

The breeze coming off the ocean was balmy. She simply adjusted the waterproof material on the ground so the collapsed poles wouldn't be sticking her in the ribs, then lay down at last. There. She was perfectly content. Who needed the tent?

She was blissfully comfortable for five full minutes. Except maybe her neck. She adjusted a wadded-up blanket under her head just as a fat raindrop fell on her face. Wind ruffled her hair. Another raindrop followed.

She squeezed her eyes closed for a moment. She was *not* going to be defeated. She got up and tried to unfold the tent, to get in the middle somehow, sandwiched between protective layers. But the rain picked up long before she finished. And by the time she was settled horizontally again, she realized she was lying in mud. She cursed the prince under her breath.

She was so not supposed to be here.

He was supposed to be snug in his tent, with three intelligent, great women, each with the pedigree and temperament to become a fantastic princess. Why couldn't he have just gone with that plan? What did he have to complain about?

"It's raining," he said from a few feet away, his rich baritone startling her.

She hadn't noticed him coming closer. "Cry me a river," she muttered through clenched teeth. Or not. They seemed to have more than enough water already. She pulled her head into her cocoon. She'd been about to get out of the mud, but she would pretend that everything was well if it killed her.

"The water running down the hillside will be heading this way," he observed with perfect aristocratic nonchalance.

Maybe it would wash him away. That could be another solution to the problem. He couldn't very well embarrass the monarchy any more if he disappeared, could he?

But the water would wash her away, too, if she stayed like this. She crawled out and was soaked to the skin the next second. "You know how to set this thing up?" She gestured toward the tent. If they had it anchored to the ground, maybe the water would run around them. The canvas was waterproof.

"Forget it." He grabbed the muddy, dripping tent,

tossed it over his shoulder and headed inland. His slight limp did nothing to detract from his powerful appearance.

She reluctantly followed him, carrying her soggy blanket. With the cloud cover thick now, and the rain coming down hard, she could see little, even with the flashlight. Once she thought she caught a moving shadow up ahead, but by the time she looked closer, it disappeared. Maybe one of the guards. Their gear and supplies had been dropped off on the other side of the island earlier. They'd probably gotten their tents up around the perimeter in time for the rain. Lucky them.

"Hello!" she called out. "We need help. We're here."

She waited, but no response came. Maybe they couldn't hear her. Or she'd only seen a bush moving in the wind.

Should have looked for the men this afternoon, instead of waiting for a boat by the beach and fighting, she thought as she pushed ahead, mud squishing in the front of her sandals and leaking out the back.

An hour of miserable marching got them to a rocky cliff wall. The famous Painted Rocks, not that she could make out any of the images in the rain and the dark. Soon blind luck brought them to an overhang that shielded them from most of the rain—if they sat far back in the rock's crevice and very close to each other.

He positioned the rolled-up tent in front of them to

block as much rain from that side as was possible. "You might want to take a minute and ponder where meddling gets you." His tone was lecturing. "I hope you're happy."

She would have been happy if she'd never heard of Prince Lazlo of Valtria. "I'm wet."

Her side was plastered to his. He was a full head taller than her, long limbs, muscles in all the right places. According to her research, he was an avid sportsman. Highly competitive, highly seductive, highly annoying. And, unfortunately, he was her cross to bear.

He relaxed his shoulders against the rock. His masculine scent of leather and motor oil reached her even through the rain. He'd probably spent his morning at the racetrack as usual.

She needed to think about something other than him, or she'd never relax enough to fall asleep. She gave that a valiant try for as long as she could. With her clothes soaked, she was cold to the bone, but she resisted moving even closer to him.

"First thing in the morning," she said when she could stay silent no longer, "we'll set up the tent and find our breakfast in the bags. I had the royal cook pack plenty of food for you and the women. If the rain stops, we can make a fire and signal for help."

He didn't say anything.

She thought of her small walk-up in Brooklyn, New York, that was mortgaged to the hilt. She couldn't fail here. If she pulled this off, she'd have enough money to throw some serious advertising out there and save her business.

The matchmakers' second rule was: *Win each client's goodwill. Only then can you work productively together.*

And she badly needed to keep this client.

Having to apologize, when she'd done nothing wrong, just about killed her, but she was willing to make that sacrifice. She had a month left to claim the exorbitant fee the Queen had promised her if she succeeded. She needed to gain Lazlo's cooperation and goodwill.

"I'm sorry. This isn't how I planned this."

Once again, he didn't respond.

But she did hear a sound, so she turned and saw his head resting on his shoulder, at what looked like an uncomfortable angle. He softly snored into her face.

And then he began leaning and sliding against her. She tried to move away, but somehow ended up on the ground, practically pinned under him.

"Your Highness!" She shoved him toward the edge of their shelter.

"Mmmm," he said without opening his eyes as he rolled onto his side.

Wedged between him and the rock, she had no room to pull away. She was practically spooning him. She had to get out of there. Except, the spot *was* comfortable. And his body heat was slowly drying her. And it was dark and scary out in the open.

She decided to stay put. For comfort's sake. She did her best to ignore that they were touching. Still, sleep didn't come easily.

Every noise the rain didn't drown out startled her. At one point, she could have sworn something big moved through the woods nearby. She could hear branches cracking, but as she waited with her breath held, nobody materialized from the darkness.

When she did sleep, her dreams were strange. She was with the prince on the beach, entangled, naked, waves licking their feet. He was kissing the sensitive skin of her neck, sending spirals of need through her body. In her dream, he wasn't the least annoying. The hands that at times molded metal at his auto factory, now caressed her breasts. She arched to press them into his palms as her nipples pebbled and begged for more. She tried to shift closer to him, but hit her head on rock.

What rock? They were making love in the surf on the beach. The sand was soft...except it wasn't. She was lying on rock. She slowly came awake.

The wetness on her feet was rain, not playful waves. She'd stuck them out of their shelter while she slept. Prince Lazlo had turned in the night, one arm under her head, his other hand cupping one of her breasts gently.

Heat rushed to her face. "Your Highness!" She squeaked the words as she tried to wiggle away from him, but the rock provided no space.

Firmly, she pushed the hand away. "Prince Lazlo, this is not—" She glanced up into his face.

His eyes were closed, his aristocratic mouth lax. He was still fast asleep.

ROBERTO SPIT SAND as he crawled out of the water, too exhausted to stand. The waves had broken their raft, taken their weapons—the makeshift knife as well as the guard's rifle—and separated the small team from each other.

He scanned the beach where he landed. Nothing but darkness and rain. He couldn't even tell if he'd reached the mainland or only another island. He rolled to his side and puked up some of the saltwater he'd swallowed. Then he flopped onto his back, letting the rain beat his face, unable to move another inch.

Endless hours passed. Each time the waves came up to lick his feet, he crawled a little higher. Then the rain stopped, the clouds cleared out and he could see two dark forms on the beach—either his men, driftwood or clumps of seaweed. He stood from the wet sand and staggered toward them, squinting his eyes to see.

He came across Marco first, shook him, pounded his back. When the man coughed up water at last, Roberto moved on to José. Then the three of them dragged themselves into the low brush that edged the narrow, rocky shoreline.

And for a while, they rested.

"Where the hell are we?" José spoke first, sounding

hoarse. Their throats were raw from swallowing too much seawater and vomiting.

"Close to a house, I hope." Marco shook wet sand from his curly black hair, looking the most chipper among the three. "A house full of food and women."

But instead of a house, the first thing they spotted once they got going was a tent, about a hundred meters or so inland.

Roberto signaled to the others, then picked up the largest stone within reach. They spread out and circled their target, caught the man inside the tent unawares. The guy had a weapon, but no time to use it before they smashed his skull in.

They stood over the body, breathing hard, adrenaline pumping, the scent of blood in their nostrils. They waited, listening. When they were sure that the man had been alone and nobody was coming, Roberto lit a lamp. He grinned as he looked around. His friends didn't call him a lucky bastard for nothing. "We have food, shelter and a gun again." Not a bad start to the day.

Marco was stuffing his face already. Crumbs rolled down his cleft chin as he made an animal-like sound.

"Give me that." Roberto snatched the rucksack away from him. He went through the contents, then tossed José a neatly packed sandwich, laying claim to the rest. He was the boss; he would hand out the food when and where it pleased him.

He took the largest sandwich for himself and bit into it with only slightly more restraint than Marco. They were safe for the moment, out of the weather and soon their bellies would be full. Nobody knew they were here. Probably nobody knew the man they'd killed was here, either. Surveying his gear, he looked like a lone hiker out camping.

But before they could settle in comfortably, a radio he hadn't noticed before came on, startling José into jumping.

The small device was hanging on a peg in a dark corner of the tent. "Station two, come in."

MORNING COULDN'T COME soon enough. Every inch of Milda's body ached. The only comfort she'd had over the long night was the heat radiating off the prince. Since their sole blanket was wet and muddy, she hadn't been able to use that for anything.

She looked around, rubbing the sleep from her eyes.

Lazlo was gone.

Thank God.

She ran her fingers through her hair. She wasn't one of those women who woke with perfect style and grace. At least she would have a little time to get herself together before she had to face him. A drowned rat had to look better than she did.

She ran her fingertips under her eyes to take off any smudged mascara. Not that she wanted to look attractive for the prince, but looking put together gave her self-confidence, and she had a feeling she would need all the self-confidence she could get when dealing with this client on this particular morning.

She crawled out from under the overhang, smoothed down her soiled, ruined clothes. Then the pictures that covered the rock wall caught her attention, the paintings that had been nothing but darker smudges in the dark night when they'd arrived here.

She'd heard of them when she'd been asking around for information on the island, trying to figure out whether it would be right for this project, but she'd had no idea what they depicted. She'd expected horses and buffalos like other nonhomicidal cavemen left all over Europe. She blanched now as she looked at scenes of wholesale murder. Blood splashed everywhere, necks cut, bellies opened. Shocked, she snatched her gaze away.

Good thing she hadn't seen the paintings the night before. They would have given her nightmares.

She stumbled away from the images, heading for the beach. The gear she'd put together, with professional help, included a number of toothbrushes and plenty of toothpaste. And breakfast. Most importantly, coffee. She'd have her first cup here, then another cup when they were back in the palace. They made the most amazing cappuccinos there, the frothy milk dusted with cinnamon.

She was one hundred percent certain that the boat would come for them today. The ladies had been angry. They'd made their point. The rescue team had to be on their way, if not already here.

But when she came out of the grove, she found the beach empty. No boat. No prince. And more alarmingly, no gear.

She swirled around. Maybe the boat had come and gone already. Was Lazlo mad enough at her to leave her like this?

"Your Highness?"

No response came, save the slapping of the waves.

"Your Highness?" she shouted more loudly as a twinge of panic squeezed her chest.

He couldn't just leave her. *He wouldn't,* she thought, openmouthed with shock, still scanning the empty beach. He was a gentleman.

In most situations.

But he did seem to have developed some sort of unreasonable dislike for her. Crazy, really, when one considered that she was here to help him. She was instrumental for his future happiness. That he wouldn't see that was most frustrating.

She was close to making him see reason, though. She was pretty sure. The two weeks with those ladies on this island would have done it. Once she got back to the palace, she needed to come up with another plan, and quickly.

She looked toward the mainland. The sunrise over the endless blue of the ocean filled the sky with pink. The scene was beautiful enough to take her breath away, but after a few moments her instincts prickled. Something didn't feel right. There was something…sinister in the air.

She shook her head. She thought that just because the prince was missing. Or maybe because she'd seen those dreadful pictures.

She ignored her prickling senses, although she'd always been proud of her keen intuition, a must in her line of work, a strong family trait. Having excellent intuition was essential in matching up couples.

Except, she'd never felt that sense of rightness when she'd considered a candidate for the prince. Not even with the three women she'd invited to the island, if she were to be honest, and the present moment seemed like the perfect time to face certain truths. She didn't feel that certain zing. Didn't see that image of the young couple leaving the church and rice flying. Didn't hear the proverbial wedding bells ring. Maybe that had been the problem to begin with.

Every time she'd looked at a woman and thought of her with the prince, the image brought only one thought to her mind: *wrong.* And she didn't have all that much time to keep looking.

She picked up a chunk of driftwood by her feet, walked to get another. Even a couple of larger pieces had washed onto the shore overnight. She could use smoke to signal for help. Not that she had any matches. Those were in the gear, which was presumably with the prince. Still, there was that Boy Scout thing of making a bow with a string and rubbing things against each other. She'd seen that once on TV. But before she could bring up in her mind's eye exactly how that was done, she saw a man bobbing in the water a few hundred feet from shore. He hadn't been there a moment before.

Then he was close enough for her to recognize Prince Lazlo. Relief flooded her. He was swimming for shore, pulling something with him. A green bag, dripping with water, she realized, when he was close enough to stand up and start walking.

Naked!

Her dreams rushed back. Her eyes went wide. Her throat constricted. Her heart put on a drum festival in the middle of her chest, the beat growing faster and faster, not slowing until he was out of the water enough so she could see that he was still wearing his underwear. *Phew.* Royal-blue boxer briefs.

Thank God for small mercies.

Not that the rest of his nakedness wasn't distracting enough. His upper torso was all lean muscles, drops of seawater running down his tanned skin. The rising sun was behind him, outlining his perfect shape.

Then her gaze dropped to the scars on his left leg.

She bit her lip. The skin was pulled together and a shade darker than the rest, white stripes going through the angry red here and there. He'd gotten trapped in a wreck at a racetrack crash and had been burned a few years back, an accident he so downplayed that, before now, she hadn't even been aware of the extent of his injuries. From what she was seeing now, he must have suffered horribly. That he was even walking had to be a miracle.

His stunning scars didn't detract anything from his

absolute masculine beauty. If anything, they gave him an edge that she imagined drew women even more. His physique drew *her,* for love's sake, and he was the last man on earth she would have ever been seriously interested in.

The first rule of matchmaking was: *Do not get involved with a client under any circumstances.*

He pulled his left hand through his dark hair to get it out of his eyes, shaking the bag with his other hand to dislodge a long strand of seaweed. His breathing was labored, as if he'd been swimming for a long time.

"What are you doing?" Had he tried to swim off the island with some of their supplies? That made no sense whatsoever.

"Saving the remains of our gear."

Her feet rooted to the spot. For a second, she couldn't move, couldn't speak. She couldn't really understand. "But—"

"The storm last night whipped up the waves. They ran farther up the beach than usual." He came over and lowered the bag to the ground at his feet.

"It's all gone?" She stared at him, still barely comprehending.

He nodded.

Disaster. Absolute disaster was all she could think.

"Can you go back for the rest?" She wasn't the best of swimmers.

He dropped to the sand, panting, stretching his muscular legs in front of him. "I've been at it for the last two hours. Everything else must have been carried far out to sea."

Her legs wouldn't hold her up. She sank down across the bag from him.

He opened the bag and pulled out ten jars of caviar—five red, five black—a dozen scented candles and a half-dozen bottles of champagne carefully wrapped in bubble bags.

She waited for more, then could have cried as he tossed the empty bag aside. She pulled it to herself and went through it again. And in one of the front pockets she found waterproof matches, one box of the two dozen she'd ordered from a camping supply store.

"Breakfast?" He held out a jar of caviar, the top already twisted off.

"No thanks." Her stomach was in a knot. No way could she put anything into it.

He shrugged and scooped some tiny, shiny, pearl-like beluga roe into his mouth. When he finished off the jar, he washed the food down with champagne. Then he lay back on the sand, his face to the sky, suddenly grinning while she did her best not to hyperventilate.

"How can you be happy at a moment like this?" she snapped at him.

He came up on one elbow—biceps bulging all over the place—and pinned her with those wicked dark eyes of his. "I have two weeks without you being able to do anything to get me married."

He was insufferable.

"You're missing your race," she pointed out, just to needle him.

He shrugged. "A little freedom might just be worth it."

She didn't say anything for a while, then, "We should light a fire and send smoke signals."

He looked over the meager pile of driftwood she'd collected. "If the guards are on the other side of the island, they won't see it. Better we save the wood for tonight to keep warm. It has to dry before we can light it anyway."

She couldn't bear the thought of another night. Under those rocks. With the prince. "The boat will come."

"Maybe. But we need a plan B."

"We should find another shelter. And we should go and find fresh water before the day gets too hot." They were in the Mediterranean. There was plenty of heat; his shorts were half-dry already. And they needed to do *something.* Sprawled on the sand, he looked like he was on vacation. He gestured toward the champagne bottles.

"That won't prevent dehydration. In fact, alcohol speeds it." Lady Szilvia, the survival expert, had told her that when she'd given advice about what to bring. And Milda had made sure to pack plenty of water. Except, those plastic bottles were now bobbing somewhere in the sea. "We need fresh water."

"We have nothing to put it in until we drink the champagne."

She hated that he had a point. "We could pour the champagne out."

He seemed to consider that, but then he said, "On the off chance that we might be here awhile without much food, we could need those calories."

She grabbed the bottle from him.

The bubbles tickled down her throat deliciously. After the ninth or tenth sip, she felt some of the tension leaving her body. "There." She took another gulp, then tossed the empty bottle onto the sand in front of him.

He picked it up with an amused look, stood and held out his hand.

She ignored him.

He walked to the bushes and came back with his clothes, a bundle she hadn't seen there in her frenetic search for him. He dressed, then slipped the waterproof matches into his pocket, packed everything else back into the bag before slinging it over his shoulder. "Let's stash this under the overhang before we go for a stroll. Wouldn't want to lose it again."

She walked after him, trying not to look at him too much. The only man she'd ever known who managed to swagger with a limp. Who did he think he was, John Wayne?

They crossed the wild olive grove, the tangy scent of the trees heavy in the air. That odd feeling returned to her again, a premonition she couldn't put her finger on, a sense of unease. Probably because they were going back to those gruesome rocks.

"So, what are those paintings about? I didn't realize Valtria's past was that bloodthirsty."

"It's not. The island was used by Etruscan priests back in the day, for their human sacrifices. Valtrians came here much later."

A shiver ran down her spine as she thought how many men and women must have died on the island over the centuries. Which would explain the bad vibes she'd been getting. By being here, they were probably disturbing some ancient burial grounds.

She tried not to look at the rock paintings as they emptied the bag and secured their meager supplies. Then they were finally heading for higher ground. The hillside wasn't too steep, solid rock in places, brittle shale in others where she had to watch her step in order not to slip. Here and there, thick woods appeared, especially close to the top, but on the bottom, the wild groves were sparse with plenty of open areas between them.

"Is there fresh water here, do you know?" She did her best to keep up with him. He was pretty fast, even with the limp.

She was wearing sandals. Only two-inch heels, but still… She hadn't planned on staying on the island beyond explaining the camping trip to Lazlo and introducing him to the ladies. She'd planned on being back at the palace by dinner, at the latest. At least she'd had the good sense to wear summer slacks, and brought a sweater in case the wind was too much on the boat ride over.

"There's a stream."

"Do you know where?"

"No idea. I was only here once, when I was a kid."

The higher they went, the denser the vegetation became.

"Wild animals?" She remembered last night's worry.

"Rabbits and foxes."

At least that was reassuring.

They walked until noon but found nothing. "We should switch tactics and walk the perimeter of the island," Lazlo recommended. "Even if the guards keep out of our way, we should be able to find one of their tents. We'd be set for supplies at least."

Exactly. Why didn't she think of that earlier? Had to be the champagne.

Downhill was a lot easier than up. She did slip a couple of times, but he always caught her easily. She didn't like when they were touching. He was the type of man a woman couldn't help but be aware of physically.

Several hours passed as they walked, keeping as much as possible to the shade of the trees. Her stomach growled.

"Should have brought some food and champagne," Lazlo said. "Sorry."

"We didn't know it would take this long."

It had to be midafternoon by the time he spotted the tent under a clump of trees and pointed it out to her.

She was so tired she could barely walk, but she broke into a run.

"Hello, we need help." She pushed through the open flap, relieved that the nightmare was over.

Then reeled back, was caught against Lazlo's wide chest. He swore softly, put his arms around her, tried to pull her back. But she couldn't move, couldn't take her eyes off the sight in front of her.

Inside the tent was the dead body of one of the guards. Lying in a pool of blood, stripped naked. A sight that eerily echoed the rock paintings.

Chapter Three

Lazlo searched for a weapon, but Ben's gun was gone. So was his radio.

"For love's sake." The mumbled words came through as Milda cupped her hands in front of her mouth. Tears filled her eyes, which were round with shock.

He looked outside. The woods seemed empty, the birds trilling in the air, no sign that anyone might be lurking in the bushes. He waited anyway, watching for any movement, listening for any sound that didn't belong. When he was certain that they were alone, he pulled the tent flap closed behind them.

"We'll be fine. I think we're alone for now. As soon as I take care of Ben, we should grab whatever we can use, then get out of here."

The young guard had only been working at the palace for a little over a year. He was a fine polo player and an antique car enthusiast. They'd had some conversations. Yesterday wasn't the first time the man had been assigned to Lazlo's personal detail.

He wrapped the man in his sleeping bag, then carried

him outside, to a spot they'd passed on their way to the tent. A storm had uprooted an ancient olive tree, leaving a giant hole in the ground. He laid Ben in the hole, then went back for the short camping shovel he'd seen in the tent's corner.

Milda still stood in the same spot, looking at the pool of blood, her arms folded in front of her, her face ashen.

He handed her their bag, the one he'd salvaged from the sea and brought along in case they found anything suitable to eat. "You should start packing." She needed a distraction.

He waited until her eyes focused on him at last and she gave a dazed nod.

Burying Ben took a fraction of the time it would have if Lazlo had to dig a hole, but still much longer than he preferred. He said a prayer as best he could, and marked the grave. His people would be back for the body, but he had no idea how many days that would take. First he had to get off the island. In the meantime, he didn't want to leave the guard to the birds and the foxes.

He wished he'd at least found Ben's radio so he could figure out where Vince, the other guard, was. Probably camping on one of the island's high points. If Ben took the shore, the other would take the highest lookout point. That would make the most sense.

Back in the tent, Milda was still standing and staring. He put a blanket in the bag she held. And he realized there wasn't much more to take. He tossed aside a pair of boots that wouldn't fit either of them. Then grabbed three books, highbrow literary novels. If nothing else, they could use the paper to start a fire.

A couple of plastic bags littered the tent's floor. He took those. Might come in handy for something. He rechecked the small tent, hoping for more, but whoever had killed Ben had cleared the place out fairly well.

At least they had their own tent back at Painted Rock. The bottom panel of this one was soaked with blood. He took the duffel bag from Milda and slung it over his shoulder. "Ready?"

For the first time ever, he hated that she was quiet. She was clearly rattled, but he couldn't give her time to gather herself. They had to get moving.

He turned to look around the campsite one last time before heading out. The grass had been trampled on and flattened. Ben had probably done a fair share of that. So had Lazlo and Milda for that matter. He could see cracked twigs and the soil disturbed here and there, a faint path leading into the woods, but couldn't tell how long it had been since anyone had walked that way, or whether it had been Ben or his killer.

Maybe Miklos or Arpad could have done better. They were the best hunters among the royal brothers. They went after elk and even bear. The most Lazlo ever did was join in the occasional fox hunt, which he did for the sake of riding. Nobody noticed his limp on a horse. He played polo for the same reason. But real sport, for him, began and ended on the racetrack.

"Who would do this?" Milda's voice trembled,

her blue eyes searching his face as she waited for an answer.

"Maybe a fugitive. Or someone who got shipwrecked and went crazy."

The island was supposed to be uninhabited. Only the odd ornithologist visited now and then, usually during the spring or fall, when migrating birds stopped to rest here. And even the ornithologists needed a royal permit to conduct their observations.

She rubbed her hands up and down her slender, bare arms. She didn't have that stunning cover model look that normally tended to capture his imagination, but she did have an earthy sort of wholesome thing going on. What they called the "girl next door" look, he supposed, and he kind of knew what that meant, although there were no girls next door to where he lived. The royal palace stood alone on Palace Hill.

At the moment, she looked frightened and fragile, but he'd fought against that steel core of hers too many times these past few months to forget that it was there. She kept looking back toward the clearing, slowing her steps each time.

He took her by the hand and led her deeper into the woods. "We need to keep moving. Whoever did this might come back."

She didn't pull away. "What about the other guard?" She seemed completely subdued. Downright meek.

He warned himself not to get used to that. She was scared, *not* reformed. "We'll find him. Don't worry about it."

She shivered. He almost pulled her closer on reflex, but he caught himself in time. Of all the women he knew, she was the one who would need comfort from a man the least. She was no shrinking violet. He had likened her to a she-dragon several times in the past, in fact.

She'd never shown an ounce of respect for his title. Every chance she got, she stood up to him. She was incredibly pushy. And when he'd tried to seduce her upon arrival, to distract her from her matchmaking, she'd resisted. Not that he was so vain that it would have bothered him. But still.

Yet the pluck now seemed to have gone right out of her. He watched her suspiciously. *Could be some new trap.* She was endlessly inventive when it came to tricking him into all sorts of things that pushed him closer to the shackles of matrimony. But try as he might, he couldn't figure out how acting meek now would benefit her.

Maybe she'd never seen a dead body before. Plus, she was a city girl. The whole nature thing was probably wearing her down, too. That thought cheered him up, so he spent some time on it. *Milda Milas subdued and malleable. Paradise at last!*

He mercilessly squashed whatever protective instincts her unusual mood brought out in him.

"I'm hungry," she said after a while, her voice still shaky. "Could we go back for food?"

She'd had nothing for breakfast but champagne.

"I'm afraid our stash of caviar will have to wait. We

need to find Vince. We need weapons and a way to communicate with the outside world."

"We can't keep walking if we don't eat." She pulled her hand from his.

To his regret, her subdued state seemed to be coming to an end. He stopped and faced her. "A person can go for days without food. You can't go nearly as long with a knife between your shoulder blades."

She paled.

Regretting his words, he drew a slow breath. "We'll come across something."

And a little while later, they did. They stopped and lunched on wild oranges that were small but plentiful on this side of the hill. The sweet juice was just the right thing to quench their thirst, while the pulp was enough to make them feel like their bellies weren't empty.

They were spending time together almost companionably. It was the strangest thing.

She sat cross-legged, her slim back against a tree, peeled her fourth orange with dainty fingers and bit in. A drop rolled down her chin before she caught it. Her lips were moist and shiny, like rubies in the noon light.

A honeybee buzzed by, circled her head. With her hair all wild, she looked like some woodland fairy. In the right light, from the right angle, she was almost pretty, he realized with some surprise. Yes, *definitely* pretty. He might have noticed it before if he weren't always trying to evade her.

The bee circled again. She swatted it away, but within

a few seconds another came by. And another. Coming from the same direction.

He pushed to his feet and walked that way, if for no other reason than because his sudden awareness of the woman, who'd been nothing but a thorn under his skin thus far, unsettled him. At the edge of the grove he found a hollow tree.

"Where are you going?" she called after him.

"For honey. Stay where you are."

He broke off a young branch, stripped the leaves then the bark with his fingernails and crept up to the tree. Very slowly he reached up and dipped the branch inside; very slowly, he pulled it out. When wild honey dripped to the ground, he grinned.

He carefully walked the loot back to Milda, who looked ready to run if they were attacked by the bees, but all they did was buzz around him. Still, a few seconds passed before she focused on the honey. But once she did, he didn't have to offer it twice. He held the branch. She put a hand next to his to steady it. Then she tilted her mouth up, and her small, pink tongue darted out to lick the sweet goo.

His groin tightened. A most unexpected reaction that jolted him.

Not possible. Not now. Not with *this* woman.

But his resolve weakened as her eyelids fluttered closed for a second and she gave a soft moan. Then she looked up at him with those dusky blue eyes. "This is beyond good. Thank you. I needed this."

He cleared his throat to respond. But as she went

back to her snacking, he forgot what he was about to say. Lost track of time there for a second.

Until she looked up at him again, sheepishly. "I ate it all."

He blinked hard and tossed the branch to the ground. He needed to snap out of it. They needed to get going and find the guard, make contact with the mainland. Instead, he hesitated.

She winced as she shot him a guilty look. "I was so hungry I wasn't even thinking."

A drop of wild honey still glistened on her lips.

He liked full, pouty lips. Hers were on the thin side and crooked when she smiled. Not particularly seductive. Nobody was more surprised than he when he leaned in.

She was soft and sweet; her mouth fitted his to perfection. He felt his body harden in a split second, his reaction disproportionate to the minor amount of bodily contact between them. He barely brushed his lips across hers, but he felt the impact all the way to his toes.

For a moment so brief that he might have imagined it, she went with the flow. Then she was pushing against him. He pulled away, searching her stunned face, trying to gather his scattered thoughts.

Her lips moved but no sound came out. She was probably looking for the words with which to best berate him.

And he definitely deserved that. What in hell had he been thinking? Her life mission was to make him miserable. Normally, he couldn't stand the sight of her.

He pulled his spine straight and stepped back, standing stiff and still.

And with that symbolic distance between them, whatever craziness had possessed him disappeared. He didn't know where it had come from, but he did know one thing for sure: under no circumstances would he ever touch this woman again. She was nothing but trouble.

"I—" She swallowed. "We shouldn't be doing this. You are—" She paused. "I am—" She made a soft noise of frustration. "We can't do this again."

For the first time they were in agreement. That threw him even more thoroughly off balance.

It wasn't right.

He weighed the issue at hand, his gaze straying to those ruby lips that were pressed into a severe, angry line. Then the solution came to him and he flashed the woman his most wicked grin. "I think we're definitely going to do this again."

And watched her sputter with outrage. Her magnificent breasts heaved with barely suppressed indignation. Her eyes were throwing thunderbolts.

Which made him relax. Everything was back to normal between them again.

ROBERTO STOLE FORWARD, breathing hard from the effort, wiping the sweat that ran into his eyes as he looked up. The top of the hill seemed a lot closer now than the last time he'd stopped for a breather. He needed high ground to see if his hunch was right and they were on an island. He wanted to know how many houses there were.

José and Marco had gone off in different directions to get the lay of the land. The three of them were to meet back in a couple of hours at the rocky beach where they'd landed.

Then Roberto reached the top at last, and could finally look around. An island, definitely. With no houses. A fishing boat passed by slowly to the north. He could see the mainland in the distance, a strip of gray at the edge of the azure.

They'd reached an uninhabited island, with two hikers. One now—whoever had spoken on that radio. Roberto scratched the stubble on his chin. Still, one was enough to spot them, to report them to the police. If they took that guy out, the island would be theirs for a few days, until people came to look for the hikers. A couple of days would be enough to recover from their near drowning. They needed rest and food to regain their strength before they made their way to the mainland. The first hiker had a considerable stash of food. And his buddy probably had supplies of his own.

The hikers had to have a boat, too, he figured. Although, so far he hadn't been able to spot it. But, between the three of them, they should be able to find the damn thing sooner or later.

He swept the vista again and thought he saw the tip of a tent by the edge of the trees to the north. He glanced at the watch he'd gotten off the first hiker. Plenty of time. And he could definitely handle one man.

He made his way down the hill, keeping the dead hiker's knife close at hand. Looked like military issue, but the man hadn't been in uniform, although his black clothes did have some sort of coat of arms on them. Maybe the two men were government surveyors of some sort.

But then, where was their equipment?

Maybe they were gamekeepers, here to keep hunters and fishermen off the island.

Roberto didn't much care one way or the other. One of them was dead, and the other was about to join his buddy.

A good hour passed before he reached the tent. He considered the gun for a second, but then grabbed the knife. With the fishing boat that close to the island, he couldn't risk someone hearing a shot.

He snuck up to the tent, burst through the flap, found the inside empty. But just then, a noise came from behind him.

MILDA MOVED ACROSS the rocky ground as if the devil was after her. They had to find the other guard. There was a killer on the island. They had no food or water, and she was getting weaker by the minute. The sooner they got to a radio the better. But that wasn't the only reason for her to hurry.

The prince had kissed her. Kind of.

Tasted her. Barely.

She'd blown the whole thing way out of proportion. She'd acted as if she'd never been kissed before. Which she had. On a few occasions. But she'd never felt that lightning of heat and need, the weakening of the knees that Lazlo's barely-there kiss had caused.

What did he kiss her for?

She pushed harder, needing to stay ahead of him and keep some distance between them.

His lips had been firm and warm and felt as good as they had in her dreams, for love's sake.

Thank God, she'd found the strength to pull away before she could completely embarrass herself. And that ridiculous threat of him wanting to do it again! She'd been marching forward in silence, rounding the island in search of the other guard ever since.

She kept going, trying to forget the kiss, trying to forget the dead guard. She had a feeling she wouldn't be able to do either. But at the very least, she had to find a way to put both out of her mind, because she had to function to stay alive.

In her haste to get away from him, she'd gotten quite a bit ahead of the prince. The sound of rolling rocks somewhere ahead of her on the hillside reached her. She couldn't see through the trees.

Could be a wild animal.

Or could be the other guard.

Or could be the killer.

She slowed, but it was too late. Since her eyes were on the woods, she didn't notice the crevasse in front of her, half covered by lush, green vines. She stepped onto the leaves, and her feet touched air. She tumbled, down, down, down, the earth swallowing her startled cry....

which ended abruptly when hitting bottom pushed the air from her lungs.

Just as well. Alerting the killer to her whereabouts was the last thing she needed.

Every part of her was sore as she stood. There were leaves in her hair and dirt on her face. Her arm stung where she'd scraped off the skin. She flexed her limbs. At least nothing felt broken.

The hole was as narrow as it was deep, probably carved by water running down the hill.

Lazlo was peering down from the mouth of the hole. "Are you okay?"

"Just get me out of here." She didn't even want to think of the snakes and spiders that were probably down there with her. Luckily, there was hardly any light filtering down to the bottom, so she couldn't see anything that would have started her screaming.

She looked up. The prince seemed to be lying down. He lowered his arm, but his hand remained out of reach. He moved forward and leaned into the hole up to his waist but, even like this, several inches still separated them.

"Can you climb up the side?" he asked.

She felt around and made contact with square stones. Maybe the hole hadn't been created by water after all. Could be that she'd fallen into an old well. She tried to climb, but the stones were covered with slippery moss and she slid back immediately. She grabbed on to some roots to support her weight, but that didn't work for long either. She jumped.

The very tips of their fingers touched.

She thudded back to the ground, panic flashing through her as dry branches snapped under her feet.

What if he couldn't pull her out of here?

Her heart beat in her throat as he disappeared from the mouth of the hole. What if he left her?

He'd disliked her from the get-go. He considered her a nuisance. She'd tricked him onto the island in the first place. It seemed unlikely that he would have forgotten that.

"Please, don't leave—" She dodged the duffel bag coming down on top of her. "What—" She scampered aside as he jumped in, nearly knocking her off her feet. "What are you doing?" Panic switched to anger. Didn't he think at all? Now they would both be trapped down here.

Instead of answering, he put a hand over her mouth and whispered into her ear, "Somebody's coming."

After a startled moment, she nodded.

He let her mouth go, but didn't step away. No place to go without rubbing against the dirt wall, roots sticking out and spiderwebs and God knew what else. Scorpions, probably. There were plenty of those on most Mediterranean islands.

But it was hard to think of the local flora and fauna when the tips of her breasts were touching his chest. The hollow of his throat was inches from her mouth. If there were more light, she could probably see his pulse beating there. She could feel his breath fanning her hair.

Last night, even being cold, wet and miserable, she'd been aware of his body lying next to hers. And then today, he'd kissed her. Now she knew how his mouth felt on hers. Their close proximity took the awareness to a whole new level.

Every time she took a breath, her breasts moved and her nipples rubbed against his chest. Heat shot through her and pooled low in her belly, as tension built. She pressed closer to him to stop the rubbing, not sure she'd improved the situation. Now her breasts were flattened against him. He put an arm around her.

She was about ready to jump out of her skin when she heard footsteps above.

They stood motionless, barely daring to breathe. Her fingers curved around Lazlo's arm. The footsteps neared, stopped. A moment passed before whoever it was began to walk away.

Then they could no longer hear him.

And with some of that acute fear gone, her full focus was back on Lazlo, against whose hard body she was plastered.

His head dipped forward.

"Don't kiss me again," she protested, then grew mortified when she realized that hadn't been his intention.

He was simply positioning himself to reach something at his back. "I haven't really kissed you yet." His voice turned low and wicked. "I was just tasting the honey."

He flipped on the flashlight and panned the sides

of the hole. Since she didn't want to look into his eyes, she kept her gaze on the walls instead.

Roughly carved, square stones peeked from the dirt here and there, their prison definitely a manmade structure. One spider that was big enough to give her nightmares for the rest of her days moved into a large crack between two rocks. She scooted closer to Lazlo, which hardly seemed possible.

He directed the light at their feet.

They were standing on old bones, most covered with moss. She couldn't even see the ground. Human, she realized when she spotted a yellowish jawbone. And about climbed the prince. *Yuck. Yuck, yuck, yuck. Oh, gross.*

"I'm guessing those would be the Etruscan sacrifices." Lazlo wasn't the least rattled. He gently peeled her off him, then bent his knees. "Get on my shoulders."

She didn't argue, for once, eager to get out any way she could. The maneuver began awkwardly, but then she thought, *to hell with it,* and grabbed on to his shoulders, stepped on his bent knee then worked herself up until she was standing with her feet next to his ears. She was just about to pop her head out of the hole when she heard a surprised shout. A man, close by.

"That was Vincent," Lazlo said beneath her. "Hurry."

She took a quick peek. Nobody within sight. She crawled out, kicking some dirt and small rocks back at Lazlo as she went. She whispered a low "Sorry."

Then Lazlo was next to her before she even began worrying about how to pull him up. He had more upper body strength than she did, she supposed. Probably could hang on to the roots more easily. He even had the bag with him.

Her gaze swept the area again as she stood. And what she saw made her heart beat faster. "Look."

A white fishing boat sliced the waves in the distance.

She waved her arms madly over her head.

"They can't see us," Lazlo said, his lips tightening. "But if we had a gun, they might hear the shots."

"We have to find Vincent."

He nodded. "Quickly."

The boat was heading away from the island.

He immediately took off in the direction of the shout, keeping himself between her and possible danger.

They walked too slowly, constrained by both the need to stay silent and the mess of vines and bushes. An eternity seemed to pass and they still couldn't hear or see the man they were seeking.

Then he stopped and swore under his breath, motioned for her to get down, behind the cover of a tree. She immediately obeyed, foreboding making her chest heavy. He crept forward, inch by inch, toward a prone body on the ground.

The black fatigues belonged to the royal guard.

Her heart lurched into a faster rhythm.

Lazlo stopped and listened. Waited. "Vincent," he

whispered after a while, and motioned for her to stay where she was while he checked out the body.

Despite the heat, she shivered behind the tree. Another body. Deep down she knew that Vincent was dead. But this time, she got herself together faster.

THIS TIME, SHE HELPED LAZLO bury the man with a knife wound in the back, and mark the grave. Then they tried to backtrack to the guard's tent, in the hope that they would find either his weapon or his radio—neither of which were with him—or at least some food for later.

"The boat is gone." She looked out over the sea when they were back at the well again.

"If there was one, there'll be others," Lazlo said.

What he didn't mention, probably to keep her spirits up, was that even if a boat did come sufficiently close to the island, they had no way of gaining the crew's attention. Her small pile of driftwood by the beach was nothing. They definitely needed to work more on that later.

But it was dusk by the time they found Vincent's campsite. His supplies were missing. At least his tent was on sandy soil, which provided some clues.

Lazlo inspected the ground carefully. "The prints are from three different sets of shoes. Only one would be Vincent's."

The implication wasn't lost on her. A shiver ran down her spine. "The killer is not alone."

"And they have weapons. Two guns now, at least. Knives."

"We could hide."

"Don't count on it. I don't know why these people are on the island, but something tells me they want the place for themselves. If they saw us land yesterday, they know that we're here. Sooner or later, we'll meet up with them. And when we do, it's either them or us," he said, laying it on the line.

Her mouth was as dry as the sand under their feet. She felt a new wave of panic wash over her, but then she steeled herself. She was no shrinking violet. She was a New Yorker. "Them," she said, without hesitation. "We need to get them before they get us." Not that she had the faintest idea how to go about that.

Prince Lazlo looked surprised for a moment. But then, for the first time perhaps ever, he flashed her a pleased grin. "That's my spunky matchmaker."

"Marital consultant," she corrected him, out of habit.

He good-naturedly nodded. "We'll go back to the Painted Rocks to spend the night there. We'll gather some oranges on the way."

"I really hate that place. The paintings give me the creeps."

"We need that caviar, and the champagne wouldn't be bad, either. If we emptied another bottle, we'd have two for water when we finally find that stream."

"Maybe we'll come across it on the way back." Just

their luck that they would find a hidden well with an ancient stack of bones, but they couldn't find water.

"There's something eerie about this island. Do you feel it?"

One aristocratic eyebrow slid up his forehead. "You should have thought of that before you booked me on a two-week pleasure trip here with three husband-hungry women."

"I was running out of time. It made me desperate."

He gave her a narrow-eyed look.

"I do feel bad about it. In hindsight," she confessed.

"You should. You're messing with my life. But I'm willing to let it go for now. We'll worry about that when we get back to the palace."

"I make most of my clients very happy." She prided herself on that. "Usually, they even invite me to their wedding. One couple asked me to be godmother to their little boy. And another named their girl after me." She didn't want him to think that she was a total loser.

"I dare say that's not going to happen with me, Milda. Why don't you quit now? Cut your losses."

"I need this assignment too badly to quit."

He gave her a questioning look, but she wouldn't elaborate. "Maybe you've been less than thrilled with me until now, but when I find you that perfect partner, you'll be happy. You'll be grateful that I tried so hard."

"And off she goes, down the track." He shook his head and turned to go, muttering a few words under his breath. Then he said, "I'll go first. I want you to follow at a distance. That way, if we run into anyone and they catch me, you'll have a chance to escape."

She wouldn't have thought of that, but it made sense, although she wasn't sure why a prince would risk his life for a commoner, a commoner who wasn't even one of his subjects. Self-sacrifice from Prince Lazlo? Not the image the media had painted of him, for sure. But maybe there was more to him than being a speed-obsessed, spoiled, womanizing prince.

They reached the wild orange grove at twilight, filled the bag and their shirts with fruit that provided both nourishment and moisture. But in all their wandering, they hadn't found any signs of the stream. Whatever else they did, the next day they had to find fresh water.

They ate more honey, then moved on. Night fell, clouds soon drifting in to cover the moon. She followed him, listening for the soft noises he made, nearly indiscernible from the noises of the forest. He was far enough ahead so that the sound his feet made on the ground barely reached her.

The footsteps she heard suddenly from behind were much louder, much closer.

Chapter Four

There were more people on the island. Roberto swore. He'd wondered about that, and followed the second hiker for a while this afternoon, hoping the man might lead them to others, if there were any. But the guy had noticed him and Roberto had to take him out. Not an easy task. For someone taken by surprise, he had put up a surprisingly good defense. Still, he wasn't a match for Roberto's prison brawl skills, skills that had taken his decades-long street fighting experience to a whole new level.

By the time Roberto got back to the man's tent, Marco had been there, rifling through the supplies.

They'd gathered up what they needed, then went to meet up with José. Then the three of them decided to bring one of the dead men's tents over and set it up, leaving behind the cave José had discovered high up the hillside. They'd spent the previous night in that place, grateful to be out of the rain. It was more easily defensible than a tent, should anyone come to the island to look for them; but the swarm of bats that returned from their night hunt at dawn had scared them.

So they'd set up the tent, then ate and rested. When twilight fell, José went on guard duty and Marco went to sleep. But Roberto was restless. He'd decided on a walk in the woods instead. And heard a man say something. A woman answered. Then they fell silent as they separated and passed through the forest. More hikers? For an uninhabited island, the place sure seemed popular.

He gripped his knife, moved closer to the woman. Then a branch snapped under his feet, and he swore silently, spotting her at last. She stopped and looked back. He remained still, in the shadow of a leafy bush. She didn't see him, and she turned back to the path.

He moved closer, watching every step, until he was close enough to lunge. He knew where the knife had to go, to hold her mouth shut so she couldn't give warning.

But as he got ready to make his move, the man strode into sight.

"Don't stay too far back. I don't want to lose you."

"I heard something," she said.

The man peered into the woods behind her.

Roberto held his breath. They were two meters from each other, impossible to miss, but for the thick vegetation and the dark of the night. The tree canopy was low, but sufficient to block out most of the moon above.

The man peered into the deep shadows, then, after a moment, shrugged. "The night noises of the forest, I'm sure. We should keep going, we're almost there."

They walked off together and soon came to the end of the woods, entering a flat and open area, where Roberto could no longer follow them unseen.

But at least, now he knew that they were here. He and his team had more work ahead of them before the island would truly be theirs.

MILDA WAS BONE TIRED by the time they reached the Painted Rocks, but she hadn't complained. She simply pushed forward and did what needed to be done. Most women Lazlo knew would have been whining for a limousine by now, to take them back to their five-star hotel.

Somehow, she managed to look more attractive without makeup and with smudges on her face, her hair all mussed. Spending the day with her, just trying to survive, was starkly different from the way they normally spent time together—her harping on him to get married and he trying to get away. Their trek across the island hadn't been bad. She'd been scared out of her wits, but held herself together. She even helped pick oranges, had offered several times to carry their bag. Had assisted in burying Vincent.

He was beginning to appreciate her company. And as much as he told himself that kissing her again would be a considerable mistake, truth was, he wouldn't have minded tasting her lips one more time, honey or no honey.

He shook his head.

Absolutely not. Not this woman.

When he'd threatened her with more kisses, he'd only said that to keep her off-kilter. He hadn't meant any of that. Definitely *not.*

Except, he was beginning to rethink the issue, once they were snuggled together for warmth under the overhang again. They hadn't dared to erect their tent. The tents of both guards had been discovered by the killers. He figured it'd be better if their shelter wasn't visible from a distance.

"We need to find water tomorrow," she said as she lay stiffly next to him.

"We'll have to be careful. If the men who killed Ben and Vincent have been living on the island for a while, they probably know the creek and use it."

She stilled. "I just thought of something."

He waited.

"When I first got the idea for your hike with the ladies, I talked with the chief of palace security."

"And he didn't talk you out of it? I'm disappointed in the man." How many people had a hand in setting him up? The sense of betrayal returned.

"He didn't know the details, just that I might be planning an event here that might involve some of the princes."

At least the man wasn't laughing behind his back.

"The point is," Milda went on, "that he sent a team to make sure the island would be a safe location for my plans. They didn't find anyone here."

"When was that?"

"Three weeks ago. But your brother Miklos also sent a group of his men the morning before our arrival, to do another sweep. He gave me the all clear."

"He should have given me a warning instead." He had a lot to say to his brothers once he was back at the palace.

"So these men must have come here after us. Maybe during the storm that first night."

"Could be their boat capsized near the island. But they are no fishermen in distress. These are killers." Again, all he could think of was the Freedom Council. More likely than the capsized boat with a couple of murderers inside, was that the men were here with a purpose, and that purpose was to kill him.

Milda had fallen silent. He decided to drop the topic. He had no way of gaining any information, and there was little sense in speculating. Nor did he want to scare her.

They listened to the noises of the night for a while, and he gradually relaxed. The stars were incredible, the moon lording over them like a king over his subjects. Milda would call him "typical prince" if he shared that thought with her, he realized, and grinned, forgetting the dangers around them.

In this moment it seemed that they were the only two people on the island, in the whole world perhaps. Far from being uncomfortable, the thought brought him an odd sort of contentment.

"Good night." She turned from him.

"Good night." He put his arm around her waist as he held her from behind.

And after a few minutes, she finally relaxed against him.

The crevice provided them with little room. They'd decided not to risk lighting a fire, so they had to snuggle together for heat. They had one blanket under them, on top of the folded tent, not that the thin layer could make them forget that they were lying on a rock bed. The lone blanket that covered them was insufficient against the chill of the night. They needed each other to be even remotely comfortable.

Their physical proximity meant nothing. At least, that was what he told himself.

"Milda?" he asked a few minutes later, just to hear her voice, which wasn't altogether unpleasant when she wasn't harping.

"Yes?"

"What kind of name is that? Is it short for something? It's not a typical American name."

"My family is Lithuanian American. My great grandparents came over on a ship, through Ellis Island." She paused, as if considering whether to say more. Then she did. "Milda is the name of a mythical Lithuanian love goddess."

He heroically held back any smart comments, saying only, "Perfect name for a matchmaker."

She wiggled around to face him. Enough moonlight spilled into the crevice to illuminate her face. "Marital consultant."

"Is that a legitimate occupation in Lithuania?"

She stiffened. "It's a legitimate occupation everywhere. I'm a certified, card-carrying member of MCA, Marital Consultants of America."

"Of course you are."

Her chin came up. "The women of my family were always in the business, one way or another. My family name, Milas, is short for Milasiniks—'love potion maker.'"

Unease crept into his mind. "You haven't—"

"I don't believe in potions. True love has to come from the heart, not from a bottle."

He normally wasn't crazy about her ideas on true love, but he appreciated this one. The last thing he needed was for a desperate matchmaker to poison him. "No potions. Promise."

She rolled her eyes. "I could be offended by all this mistrust."

"We're trapped on this godforsaken island because you tricked me," he reminded her. "Trust is not going to come easily."

At least she looked contrite for a fleeting second. "Fine. No potions. I promise. Are you happy?"

Not exactly, but as he lay next to her, his gaze straying to her crooked lips, he realized that it wouldn't take much to make him at least a little happier than he was at the moment. She had surprised him today. Not many women had ever done that. He'd seen another side of her, and this other side was…not at all like what he'd seen of her at the palace. She had gumption. She had common sense. She sucked it up and toughed it out when things turned bad.

If he wasn't careful, he was going to develop some misplaced admiration for her.... All right, probably not. That would be going too far. But there was some draw between them, for sure.

As he thought of their kiss in the orange grove, he could still taste the wild honey, and his head dipped forward without conscious effort. Her eyes went wide as their lips met.

Soft.

Sweet.

Not two adjectives he would have ever used in connection with Milda before, but there it was. He caressed her upper lip with his, then the lower, pressing kisses to the corners of her mouth.

One minute, her hands were between them, pushing him away. The next her eyes drifted closed as she capitulated. And what had begun as a lazy exploration turned serious all of a sudden.

Hot need shot through him as he gathered her tighter into his arms. The chaste tasting of her lips seemed woefully inadequate. So he deepened the kiss, his body waking up all over as she let him in.

All the tension, fight and fire that had built between them in the past five months, that whole giant ball of energy transformed in that moment, and the intensity of the desire he felt left his hands shaking.

That sobered him up.

He didn't even like her, for heaven's sake. Her job

was to make his life miserable. And so far, she had succeeded splendidly. What would she do if he gave her any kind of power over him?

He pulled away, his body reluctant to follow his mind's direction.

"Okay," he said, then cleared his throat to get the hoarseness out of his voice. "I'm not certain what's going on here, but it's not going to keep happening. You were right. We shouldn't do this. Ever again." His body loudly protested, but he ignored his baser instincts with the aplomb of a prince.

She was pulling back, too. Not that she had far to go. The small crevice only allowed an inch or two between them. Her warm breath still fanned his cheek. "Absolutely." The first word came out a little dazed, but then she recovered herself. "It's wrong. You're my client." A note of desperation snuck into her voice. "There are rules. I never should have— Could we please pretend this never happened?"

"That would be best."

They both stayed quiet after he said that. Another rare occurrence of agreeing on something. He suspected that neither of them knew what to do with this unexpected harmony.

"Why is this happening now?" she asked after a while, sounding frustrated.

What was he supposed to say to that? He had no idea why his body suddenly noticed her and wanted her. But he wouldn't make another move if it killed him. "Desert

Island Syndrome," he said as nonchalantly as he was capable.

Her eyes narrowed. "That's not too flattering."

"Neither of us is thinking rationally."

She nodded in agreement. "The important thing is that we seem to have come to our senses."

"Exactly."

Another stretch of silence followed.

"Tomorrow we figure out where those bastards are. We need to get one of the radios back from them, at least." He was the first to speak this time, needing to get his mind on another track so his body would calm down.

"Where do you think they are?" Milda obliged him, seeming just as anxious to forget that kiss.

"There are caves and Etruscan ruins on the other side of the hill."

More silence. Then her hand came up as she touched his arm lightly. "I'm sorry I've put your life in danger. It's the last thing that I wanted." She sounded sincere.

"Don't worry about it. This is Valtrian land. Those criminals are not going to claim it. I'm going to take care of them." He paused for a second as he thought of something. "You do realize that my brothers will actually be jealous of the adventure when I get back to the palace and tell them?"

A ghost of a smile played on her lips as she retrieved her hand. "And yet they seemed so sane."

"My brothers? You must not have looked too closely."

But *he* was looking closely. At *her.*

And he had to stop doing that before he forgot his resolution of not touching her again. Because every cell in his body still wanted her.

He did the only thing he could think of, and turned his back to her. "Good night," he called over his shoulder.

"Good night," she responded on a sigh behind him.

Then something rattled in the woods and she was plastered against his back again. "What was that?"

He listened, but the sound didn't come again. "Probably just the wind." He closed his eyes. Not that he expected to get any sleep, with her breasts pressing against his back. He fancied he could even feel the nipples.

Chapter Five

Milda soaked up the heat Lazlo radiated and wished she could sleep. She wouldn't have moved away for anything. She needed the reassurance of his nearness.

Cloud cover made the night too dark to see beyond a few feet. Tree branches rubbed together in the woods, moved by the breeze coming off the ocean. Now and then bugs chirped nearby. Or the screech of an owl interrupted the silence. She kept listening for other kinds of noises, those that would tell her if someone was out there.

The night before, her biggest problem had been the rain and Lazlo's fury at being stranded on the island. Amazing how much could change in just twenty-four hours. Two people had been killed. And the killers were somewhere on the island.

Forget sleep. She was too scared to even close her eyes. The rocks under their bedding dug into her side. She shifted. Sighed. She'd come to Valtria to save her business and get her life back on track. She didn't want to die here, like some sacrifice to the Etruscans.

"Are you all right?" Lazlo asked, without turning.

"Can't sleep."

"Stop thinking."

"Sure." If only it were so easy. "Those men are probably sleeping for the night. Right?"

"Of course they are." He didn't sound convincing. "Think about something else."

His nearness and kisses came to mind, but she didn't want to think about that, either.

"So everyone in your family is a matchmaker?" he asked after a minute, to distract her.

"Marital consultants. All seven of my sisters. If I can't make this work, they'll be coming over to help me," she said matter-of-factly. "We've been e-mailing almost every day."

He gave a choked sound that made her smile into the darkness. But then she felt bad for putting him on. It had been partially her fault that they were here on this island, in danger, in the first place.

"Take it easy. I'm an only child. The only Milas left, actually. I *am* the family," she confessed.

"What happened to the rest?"

"My parents died in a train accident when I was four. They were visiting Lithuania. Kaunas, where my family is from." She barely remembered them, which bothered her a lot. She clung to the few hazy memories. A visit to the zoo and her fourth birthday party were pretty much all she had. "My grandmother raised me. She passed away a couple of years ago."

Her grandmother had been the one to tell her about

her parents' death, had shown her the city of Kaunas on the map. She hadn't understood how her mother and father could have died on that piece of paper, kept looking behind it to see if they were there. To this day, the sight and sound of an unfolding map filled her with anxiety.

"I'm sorry," Lazlo said.

He probably couldn't imagine what it was like to be truly alone. He had a large family; and a prince would never be alone, anyway. The palace staff numbered in the hundreds.

"What's it like to have five brothers?"

"I'm reevaluating my feelings about that, since mine saw fit to set me up."

"They were only trying to help."

A groan was his only response.

"Must have been great growing up."

"You cannot underestimate the trouble we got into."

She didn't have a hard time picturing that. Although the Kerkay princes always behaved impeccably in public, there was something about them that suggested they could raise considerable hell if they put their minds to it. Those lively dark eyes they'd inherited from their mother had plenty of mischief and sparkle in them. There was Lazlo, for example. The paparazzi didn't call him "the Rebel Prince" for nothing.

"Who was the worst?" she asked, although she had her own suspicions.

He thought for a second. "I was the loudest for sure.

And the quickest. Took everything for a joyride, from the golf carts when I was six, to the royal ceremonial limousine when I was eight." There was a smile in his voice. "I think Istvan did the most damage. He was always quiet, but rather destructive. He always fancied being an archaeologist. I don't know how many times he dug up the palace gardens. And if he ever got his hands on any tools left lying around, he would hide in some quiet corner and go to work on the wall. One time, he caused a collapse in the royal chapel. He always wanted to know what was under and behind everything. Even back then, in his own mind, he was this great explorer."

Istvan was so reserved and withdrawn, she laughed out loud at the picture of him as the budding Indiana Jones of Valtria.

"Don't laugh. He ended up becoming a cultural anthropologist, and goes on digs every chance he gets. He's made some incredible discoveries in Valtria and abroad. You probably heard of those thirteenth-century royal graves up north." Warmth and pride came through Lazlo's voice; he obviously loved his brother. "I'll take you when we get out of here, if you haven't seen them yet."

For a moment, she was stunned by what he was saying. That he would want to spend time with her without being forced to. Normally, he did his best to avoid her at the palace.

"Actually, you should work on matching Istvan, not

me," he said thoughtfully. "I don't have any trouble getting my own dates."

That last bit was the truth and then some, even if he only said it to get rid of her. "I hardly think Istvan would have trouble getting a date if he wanted one. He's just focused on his work." He was just as handsome as the rest of the brothers. "I'd have a hard time believing that the ladies of the court aren't standing in line to go to dinner with him."

"He prefers people who've been dead for a few centuries. His nanny is to blame. The woman read him nothing but books on history and the adventures of famous explorers. She was the biggest know-it-all. I used to feel sorry for him."

"Who was your nanny?" She could easily picture him as a child who was more than a handful.

"A former model. A very distant cousin who got the job as a favor. She shaped my tastes considerably."

I'll just bet, she mused.

"How about Arpad?" That one looked as remote and withdrawn as Istvan on the few occasions that she'd seen him.

"Arpad was the big brother who taught us everything. And Miklos was born for the military. Even as a little kid, he always played soldier," he reminisced.

She didn't envy his wealth or power, but just a little, she did envy his family. The princes were really something. She couldn't remember ever seeing this many strong, honorable, outrageously gorgeous men all in one pack. The women of Valtria must have walked around in a continuous daydream.

Lazlo shifted next to her, causing the blanket to slip off. She reached out to cover herself again, her hand briefly brushing against his chest.

And because she was so ridiculously aware of even that small contact, she forced herself to focus on something else. Like his childhood. Maybe thinking of him as just a little boy would help. "So, did you ever crash any of the vehicles you misappropriated?"

He made a noise in his throat. "Are you trying to insult me?"

ROBERTO WALKED into the tent and caught Marco hiding something under his shirt. He glanced around. Nothing obvious was missing. The pile of food at the head of his sleeping bag looked undisturbed.

The tent provided cramped quarters for the three of them, but they made do. Only two slept at a time, anyway. One was always on guard—José was due to come in, and Marco was supposed to take over.

Still, the tent could have been bigger. He could always kick Marco out. Especially if the little bastard kept stealing food. Marco could go back to the cave where they'd spent the first night. Unease skittered down Roberto's spine at the thought of the cave. He hated bats. As perfect as the damn cave would have been for a hiding place, he was unlikely to go back there. Cramped or not, he preferred the tent.

"Hey, boss. I'm ready to go play night guard," Marco

said, with a little too much enthusiasm, stepping toward the exit.

Roberto blocked his path, keeping his right hand near the gun tucked into his belt. "What have you got there?"

"What are you talking about, this?" Marco pointed to the blanket at his feet. He scooped it up. "José said the mosquitoes were killing him out there, so I came back to grab it up. You want it?"

"What's under your shirt?"

Marco paled. "Nothing."

Roberto waited. Held his left hand out after a few seconds.

Marco's lips tightened, hate narrowing his eyes as he handed over two black leather wallets.

Where the hell did these come from? He didn't have to ask the question. Marco must have lifted them off the dead men. Roberto flipped one wallet open, then the other, saw the money with some disappointment. Valtrian currency. He would have preferred euros, that they could have used once they reached the mainland.

Then his eyes fell on the ID. *Valtrian Royal Security.*

For a second or two, he couldn't figure out what this meant, what those men were doing here. Why would "royal security" guard an inhabited island? Then he felt a smile spread on his face. "Find José and get ready. There is another man and a woman on the island."

"Do we have to go now? How long is this gonna take?"

"We'll go now and keep looking till we find them," Roberto snapped, dropping his voice into a warning growl. "And if you ever take anything without telling me again, I'll cut you open." He was on the younger man instantly, his knife at his throat, up against his Adam's apple.

Marco's eyes went wide as he stumbled back.

Roberto grabbed him by the arm and shoved him toward the opening of the tent. "Be ready to go in two minutes."

SHE WOKE TO THE SUN caressing her face and remembered only remnants of the stories Lazlo had entertained her with during the night. She loved it when he talked about his family. The love was palpable in his voice. Made her wonder what it would have been like to grow up knowing her parents, have siblings….

Whether intentionally or not, he'd done a good job of distracting her from her fears and setting her mind at ease. The awareness between them never did lessen, but she'd fallen asleep anyway, once she became completely exhausted.

Now she was alone again, like the morning before. Then, as she crawled from their shelter, she spotted the prince sitting on a rock not far from the crevice, surveying the sea.

The very last of her dreams still lingered. Of him. Kissing her again. She stifled a groan, but had a hard time putting the images and sensations out of her mind, couldn't shake the way he'd made her body feel. She'd never been this aware of a man before. This must be what people called blind lust. All he had to do was look at her and a zing went through her body.

It was exciting, but she would have appreciated if the source of her body's awakening had been anyone but the prince.

"Good, you're awake," he said, without turning. "Come look at this."

She finger-combed her hair and rubbed the last of the sleep out of her eyes, adjusted her pants and top, which were hopelessly wrinkled at this point. Then she walked up behind him, doing her best to forget her dreams. "What are we looking at?"

"There." He pointed.

And she saw, at last, a small, square shadow under the surface of the sea, at the rocky edge of the beach. "Is that…"

"One of our supply bags got stuck among the rocks. I didn't want to leave you here alone. Get ready as fast as you can. Before a wave washes it out to sea."

Her heart immediately thrilled. She practically ran into the bushes to complete her morning toilet. She was finished in under two minutes.

"Have you seen the others, the men who…" She couldn't finish.

Lazlo was covering their sleeping nook with some leafy branches. "No movement so far. They're probably on the other side of the island."

She hoped they would stay there until she and the prince had a chance to recover their bag from the sea.

They needed some real food desperately. Plus they needed to find that creek. And one of the radios the criminals had taken. Sure looked like they were going to have a busy day.

Which was fine with her. The less time she had to think about the prince's kisses the better. Because, now that her mind was fully awake, she was remembering that not all contact between her and Lazlo had been in her dreams.

The prince *had* kissed her.

And even he couldn't claim, this time, that it hadn't been a real kiss.

Thank God he didn't seem inclined to bring up the issue this morning. She would have died of embarrassment.

She'd about melted in his arms, forgetting all her reasons to resist. She had lost all ability to think, could only feel a fiery need that she had never felt before with any man. And she'd been willing to forget all the rules she had lived by until now. She would have been willing to give up everything.

But not him.

He had coolly pulled back. "Desert Island Syndrome," he'd called it.

And she called herself a hundred kinds of fool for falling for that kiss.

It wasn't going to happen again, he'd promised.

Damn right it wouldn't. Not if she had anything to say about it.

Temporary setbacks or not, she had to see the prince married. Her business and the rest of her life depended on it. She hadn't lied when she'd said she had appreciative clients. But not enough. These days, most of the people who came calling were mothers and grandmothers, asking for her help with their offspring. But today's young people didn't want to be married. They wanted to "hook up." They wanted to keep their options open. And as the years went by, Milda had to admit that she was part of a dying breed.

Hardly anyone believed in true love anymore. Few people wanted "happily ever after." For the short-attention-span generation, a lifetime with just one person didn't seem all that appealing.

She needed to succeed with Prince Lazlo. She needed it badly.

She followed him down the hillside, looking behind every few minutes. When they walked by a wild orange tree, she broke off the tip of a branch, chewed it up a little and used it for a toothbrush on the go.

They could have gotten down to the beach faster, but they walked slowly, making sure not to make too much noise, and stopped every once in a while to listen to see if anyone might be following.

"Stay in the cover of the bushes," Lazlo told her when they finally reached the sand. "We shouldn't both be out in the open."

"I don't want to separate. You might need help in the water."

He considered her for a moment. "All right. Let's make a run for it."

They did, choosing the shortest path to the large

pile of rocks that edged the sandy beach. Some were as big as nine or ten feet tall, others were the size of an overgrown otter. They got behind them and down as fast as they could, easing into the water.

The bag that had been easy to see in the clear, shallow sea from above was now harder to find among the rocks. But Lazlo did spot it after a few minutes. It was in deeper water. Not too deep, but above their heads, which complicated things.

He went under first, tugged at the bag. Came up for air. "Wedged in tight."

Made sense. That was why the waves hadn't washed it out to sea.

She went under to help him.

Trouble was, the bag was zipper side down, so they couldn't even open it.

They came up for air again.

"Hope whatever is in there wasn't ruined by water and we're not doing this for nothing," Lazlo was saying.

"I had to arrange for food that'd last you and the ladies two weeks without refrigeration. A lot of it is canned. The rest was sealed in airtight containers."

He gave an approving nod before going for another try. He was a stronger swimmer than she was, so it took her a few seconds to catch up with him.

He pointed to the bag then to her. Then he pointed to one of the rocks and to himself. Okay. She got it. He was going to roll the rock and she was to pull the bag.

She put all her strength into it, her lungs bursting.

Then the rock did move, and Lazlo was there helping her. Between the two of them, they dragged the bag toward the surface without much trouble.

She grinned at Lazlo and he grinned back. For the first time since they were left behind on the island, she was feeling optimistic. The food in the bag might last them a full week. Surely, help would come by then. She couldn't believe no boat had come for them yet. The ladies were taking their revenge too far. Maybe she'd been wrong about their character.

Then her head broke the surface and the first thing she heard was people talking.

"Where the hell are they?" a deep voice asked.

Another man answered him in a language that sounded Spanish. Or maybe Portuguese.

Definitely not a search crew that had come to save her and the prince.

"They went this way. Look at the footprints in the sand."

Lazlo grabbed her and pulled her tight against the rocks. She grabbed his arm as the sound of the men came nearer. They were walking onto the rocks. Before long, she and Lazlo would be seen.

He let her go and went under. He only broke the surface long enough to take a deep breath when he came back. Then he grabbed her and took her with him under the surface of the water.

She had to trust him against her most basic instincts. Since she was a poor swimmer, she didn't feel all that comfortable in the water. Going under scared her. But she followed him.

They came out just as her lungs began to ache, in a small crevice created by the haphazardly piled rocks. Their bodies were submerged, but at least they were breathing.

"Maybe they went for a swim," the deeper voice said.

A short response came in whatever language the other guy was speaking.

Something large moved next to her head. She nearly screamed. A moment passed before her eyes better adjusted to the semidarkness, and she realized that a turtle was wedged between the rocks that were covered with sea moss and even some clam shells here and there. Wedged tightly. The poor thing looked half-dead.

She signaled with her head toward the turtle.

Lazlo nodded.

Shoes scraped above.

Didn't seem like the men were going anywhere. Probably decided to wait out her and Lazlo until they came back from their supposed swim.

They could stick around for a while.

The muscles in her chest squeezed together tightly. She looked around the hole, realizing, all of a sudden, that their small shelter might not hold out that long. They were trapped in the water with barely enough room to breathe. What on earth were they going to do when the tide began rising?

Chapter Six

The men stuck to the beach and the grove, looking for a boat that might have been stashed among the trees. One of them spent an hour by the rocks, gathering clams. Only the merciless noon sun chased them away. By the time Lazlo and Milda could come out of hiding, they were weak with hunger and thirst.

The breeze coming off the sea was negligible. Coming from the shade of the rocks, the open air felt ten degrees hotter. A bigger wave washed over their heads. Even that felt balmy.

"The tide?" Milda sputtered, her eyes going wide, her wet lashes sticking together.

Had she been worried about that? No wonder she'd looked half scared to death. "Not until late afternoon. Keep down," Lazlo whispered over the sound of waves slapping against the rock and the cries of the seagulls circling above. "I'll get that turtle out." He hated to see anything or anyone trapped.

The loggerhead expressed his reluctance by sinking its horny beak—thicker than most other turtles', made to crush clam and crab shells—into Lazlo's hand. If it had been a fully grown animal, weighing more than its rescuer, Lazlo could never have managed. But a juvenile at only half a meter long, he could handle. The way the loggerhead was wedged in, he could only grab it from the front, which meant he had to keep his hand in harm's way. He did what he had to, ignoring the repeated attacks.

He freed the ungrateful thing at last and it immediately disappeared underwater. Lazlo watched it swim out to sea, then he came up next to Milda.

For the first time since they'd met, she was looking at him with approval in her eyes. Her smile was genuine, pleased—not the supercharged, let's-be-positive, this-will-work smile that was one of the tools of her trade. Her hair hung wet around her face, not a trace of makeup had remained; but beyond that smile she needed no enhancement. Even her crooked lips looked tempting. But, too quickly, she moved toward the beach, assuming they were ready to head back.

He caught up to her. "They'll be watching for us there." The men could still be close by. The fact that no voices came from the direction of the beach meant nothing. They could be taking a nap in the shade.

"Where can we get out?"

"How are you doing?" His body was weakened by the water, his muscles stiff from standing still for hours. She had to feel the strain, too. Although her body, with her clothes floating around her—allowing him a glimpse at her lace bra—looked more than fine to him.

"I'll do what I have to."

He raised his gaze to hers with effort. "This way."

On their left, the flat, sandy beach stretched for several hundred meters. On their right, the water met a rocky shoreline that was higher than the surface of the sea. He moved in that direction. If they swam close enough to the rocks, they wouldn't be seen by anyone on the shore. Once they'd swam far enough, they could climb out.

"What happened to your hand?" Her forehead wrinkled with concern when he brought the hand above water to grab on to a rock they were rounding.

"Unappreciative turtle." Red dripped into the water. Unfortunate, but they would have to swim. No way to keep that hand out. And no sense in worrying about something he couldn't help. "Be careful that the waves don't bang you against the rocks," he told Milda instead. "Some of them look sharp."

But she seemed to be considering something else. "Sharks?"

"It's a possibility."

Although, the only marine life they'd seen so far were the small, colorful fish that swam under the rocks, checking them out while they'd waited. And, of course, the ungrateful turtle.

"Keep your eyes open." He led the way, steering her clear of the most dangerous areas. If there were any strong currents or an undertow, he'd encounter it first and would have time to warn her. Not that they could put much distance between each other. Since they needed at least one hand to swim, plus a way to carry the hefty bag, they each hung on to a handle with their other hand, connected.

The first hundred feet or so went fine. Then the rocks became taller, steeper, the waves crushing against them harder. He banged his left shoulder at one point, but didn't break it, didn't even cut the skin, which was a miracle. He helped Milda through the rough spot, trying to ignore her trim body when she clung to him for a moment before she pushed forward.

They put all their focus and energy into battling the rocks and waves, but their progress was painfully slow. At least an hour must have passed before he estimated that they would be far enough from the beach so that it was safe to come out of the water.

He climbed up onto the rocks first, looked around, noted the dry brush a hundred feet or so ahead. Not much, but enough for cover. He went back, tossed the bag up, then helped Milda out of the water.

And tried not to look.

The thin material of her clothes was plastered to her body. The soggy material of her pants outlined the *V* of her thighs suggestively. She might as well have been naked. Her breasts made him ache, his fingers itching for the gentle swell of her hips. She had better curves than a top-of-the-line race car.

She pulled her clothes away from her skin and shook her legs, one after the other, like a dog, then moved on, having no apparent idea how tempting she looked, how erotic.

He kept his gaze averted as they dashed to cover, keeping down, and made their way farther and farther away from the shoreline. He led the way to higher ground, to the edge of yet another wild olive grove. From that vantage point, they would at least see if someone was approaching from below.

"Here is good," he said, and they both collapsed to the ground next to the bag.

She went through the contents immediately, not wasting any time. "Canned food, and some salmon."

That explained why the bag was so heavy.

She pulled out peaches first. "How are we going to open it?"

He searched for a small, sharp rock, then for a heavier one to use as a hammer. He managed to punch a hole in the top on the first try. He handed the can back to her. "Drink."

And she did, hungrily, dribbling the juice in through her parted lips. Lips that went crooked when she smiled. Lips that he'd tasted.

Again, he looked away. That he was becoming obsessed with her mouth was absolutely ridiculous. She wasn't even remotely his type. It had to be the island—or the heat. There was something strange going on with him.

He could understand liking her personality better, now that he'd had a chance to get to know her and she wasn't hunting him. But the sudden physical attraction was baffling.

Desert Island Syndrome.

That was what he'd told her, and he was sticking with it.

She swallowed one more time then stopped, with some reluctance, to hand him the syrupy juice. He drank a few mouthfuls, leaving a little more for her. Then, when they were done with the juice, he picked his rocks back up and set to getting to the fruit. It was a good start, but they needed protein. So he opened the shrink-wrapped smoked salmon next, and watched her inhale it while he feasted on a container of rare clams in truffle sauce, at which she only wrinkled her nose.

When they finished eating, they started back up the hill, taking the empty cans with them. No sense in leaving a trail, and they might need the containers for something.

"Might as well look for that creek while those men are lurking by the beach," she said.

"I doubt they're still there." He picked his way carefully over the loose soil. "They would have realized by now that we can't still be out there swimming."

"What will they do next?"

"If I were them, I'd round the island. They know where we went into the water. But we didn't come out there. So they're probably looking for where we came out. Then they could track us."

"Can they?" Alarm widened her eyes.

"I made sure we kept to rocky ground. No footprints."

Even here, on the side of the hill, they would be fine. The area was covered with loose gravel and brittle shale, their shoes leaving no trail.

He considered how long it would take these men to find them on this small island. It depended on how well they knew the place. "You said security checked the island over before giving the go-ahead for this trip?"

"Prince Miklos's soldiers were here all morning, to make sure the place was safe for you and the ladies. He insisted that his team would be used for this task, and no other."

Which didn't surprise him. Miklos was an army colonel and dealt with security issues regularly. "So these killers definitely came here after the island was cleared."

"Lucky timing? Just when you were supposed to arrive?" She looked skeptical.

Not more so than he felt. "The Freedom Council."

She blanched. "I thought that was finished. The rebellion was put down."

"But the Freedom Council was never caught. Maybe they're regrouping." He moved forward, his mind turning furiously, more and more questions filling it. "How many people at the palace knew about your plans for the island?"

"A handful. Only those who absolutely had to know. I had to make sure nobody told you." She winced.

Never mind that now. "But at least two dozen people know about my planned hike with my brothers. There wasn't any reason to keep that all hushed up, beyond basic security. A lot of the palace staff knew about the trip."

"And one of them could have betrayed you."

"The Freedom Council thought that all six princes would be here on this deserted island, with nothing but a few guards for protection. So they sent their assassins in."

She swallowed at the mention of the word *assassin.* He immediately regretted saying it. There was no point in scaring her. Those bastards weren't going to get to her. He was going to make sure of it.

"Why is the Freedom Council so set against the royal family? I heard bits and pieces about the rebellion, but I haven't had time to find out more."

"Too busy torturing me?" He tried to set a lighter tone.

"Too busy trying to help you." She glared.

He shook his head. Their ideas of what would have been helpful for his life were diametrically opposite.

"The Freedom Council wants the country," he explained in the most simple terms. Since there was a good chance that her life was being threatened by them, at least she should know why she was hunted all over the island. "Three prominent businessmen came up with it. They think if they do away with the monarchy, they can split the country up along ethnic lines."

"The three major ethnic groups? Italian, Hungarian and Austrian?"

Surprise sent his eyebrows up his forehead. "Good to know you didn't just hastily throw yourself into making my life miserable, but actually did some homework beforehand."

"I came to *help*." She paused. "Why is it good for them to split up the country?"

"They would each have full control over a small republic. Write their own laws. Do as they please."

"And what would happen to the monarchy?"

"The monarchy would be dead." He stopped for a moment to look around, then pointed east. "That way."

"Why? And what do you mean dead?" Her voice thinned.

He nodded toward the beach where they'd last heard those men. "Dead, as in not as fast as the assassins. And we're going this way because the vegetation is lusher up ahead. Might mean we're getting closer to the water."

"But why do they have to kill the royal family? Couldn't you abdicate or something? Why can't you just give up the throne?"

Her question set his teeth on edge. The Freedom Council had done its best to portray the royal family as dinosaurs, outdated, having no use, desperately clinging to power.

"We would, if that was what was best for Valtria. Fragmenting the country, pitching ethnic group against ethnic group, fracturing what industry we have, is not the way to a prosperous and peaceful future for the people."

"But some of the people think so."

"The Freedom Council has plenty of money to

spend on propaganda. And there are always people who are discontented with their lives. It's easy to convince them that someone else is to blame for all their misfortunes."

"But the royal weddings of Miklos and your twin, Benedek, brought the people together. And yours would give even more reason to celebrate. For a while, it would distract the people."

He blinked at her.

"Chancellor Egon told me that."

"No kidding. The chancellor is hell-bent on marrying off all the princes. It's easier than having to come up with a more serious plan, that would actually work for the long term. I'm afraid the man doesn't live up to his predecessor."

"A temporary solution is better than no solution at all." Not surprisingly, she stuck to her guns. For a matchmaker, the best solution for all the world's problems was probably marriage. "You could cooperate."

He shook his head, not expecting her to understand, but feeling compelled to try to make her see reason. "My life is not a circus act. I'm not here to distract the people from the real problems the country is facing. The chancellor needs to come up with a better solution."

"The Queen also wishes to see you wed."

"She wishes to see all her sons wed. What mother doesn't? She wants to see a roomful of grandchildren before—" He couldn't finish the sentence.

A moment of silence passed between them.

"How sick is she?" Milda asked.

For a while, he didn't answer. The Queen's state of health was a private matter. But then he ended up saying, "Sicker than the public realizes."

Milda startled him by giving him a hug. Too brief. She quickly drew back with a nervous smile. "Would it be so bad to set her mind at ease by settling down?"

He responded on reflex. "You're asking me to give up what little freedom I have left. I won't be trapped." He'd been trapped before. In a burning car. His worst fear was that he'd end up in a bad relationship, an entrapment that would last forever.

"You're a prince." She gave an incredulous laugh. "You have all the freedom in the world. You can do anything."

If only that were true. At the moment, for example, he wanted to kiss her. Since the moment he'd tasted that wild honey on her lips back in the orange grove, all he'd wanted was to kiss her again.

"Ninety percent of my life is choreographed," he said, telling her the truth. "Protocol above everything."

She watched him for a minute, looking incredulous. "What is it that you think you can't do?"

A great many things, he thought; but he gave her one that had nothing to do with her. "I can never be a professional race car driver, for one." The only thing he'd ever wanted to be, since as far back as he could remember.

Protocol wouldn't allow it. The racing associations wouldn't allow it. They couldn't handle the liability. His schedule couldn't handle it. Being a top driver took 110 percent. So did being a prince.

They reached an area of thicker grass, then bushes, then trees at last. And then finally, he could hear water trickling somewhere up ahead. He quickened his steps. They reached the water within fifty meters, a crystal-clear creek that was smaller than he'd remembered—maybe two meters wide and about thirty centimeters deep in the middle. It'd been a dry summer.

"Oh, God, we so needed this." She splashed water on her face and neck, getting her top partially wet all over again.

The creek rushed along over the rock bed—mossy in the areas of deep shade—tufts of water grasses edging the bank. He rinsed the peach can and filled it with water, wishing they had their empty champagne bottles. No matter. They would bring those back later.

She leaned to the surface of the creek and quenched her thirst from her cupped palms.

He did the same.

They looked at each other when they leaned back, satisfied, mirroring the smiles on each other's faces.

Clear droplets of water hung from her eyelashes. The sun filtering through the trees above bathed her face in soft light. *This is what Milda, the Lithuanian goddess of love, must have looked like on her best days,* he thought as warmth spread through his body. *Nothing to do with her,* he told himself.

The midafternoon heat was nearly unbearable, even by the creek. Here the air was a few degrees cooler than on the open hillside, but the humidity was getting to them. And the saltwater that had dried on his clothes and skin made him itchy. He pulled his shirt over his head.

She looked away.

Was she as aware of him as he was of her? It didn't seem possible. She'd never been anything but vocal about what she thought of him and his ways with women. And that angered him all of a sudden. What right did she have to judge him? What did she know about his life? So what if he acted out now and then? Being a prince was anything but easy. She was lucky to have been born into an average family and allowed to lead a normal life.

Well, perhaps not exactly *average.*

"Did you always want to be a matchmaker?" he asked.

"Of course," she said without hesitation, but there was something in her voice and in the way she wouldn't look at him.

"Maybe not," he observed, and thought about it for the first time. Maybe she was as bound by family expectations and traditions as he was. "You never wanted to be anything else?"

"What kind of question is that?" she snapped, with more heat than was warranted.

"A reasonable one." He watched her more closely now. "Why did you become a matchmaker?"

"Marital consultant," she said, emphasizing each word. "My mother was one."

"You barely knew your mother."

"My grandmother was one."

"And you felt like you owed her carrying on the family tradition because she raised you."

"Oh, that's good. What are you, a shrink now?" She stood and hopped over the creek in two graceful steps, anger clear on her face. "Analyze this—have you ever thought about what you're running from when you're running from a serious relationship?"

"That's ridiculous. I never ran from anything in my life."

"Maybe you drive away, then. As fast as you can, around and around the racetrack. Except, you're not getting anywhere."

"I don't want to get anywhere. I want to be at the racetrack. Have you even thought of where you'd really like to be?"

"Butt out of my life. It's none of your business."

"Where did I hear that before? That's right, I think I've told you that a time or two." *Or a hundred.*

"It's not the same." She looked thoroughly exasperated, which made her even more beautiful.

"Don't like the tables turned?" He wasn't seriously arguing with her, but would have liked to make her see his point, just for once.

"You're impossible. I'm not talking about this." She marched into the bushes on the other side, with one last murderous glance.

He'd hit a sore spot, apparently. Maybe she didn't really want to be a matchmaker after all. Could have fooled him. She'd always seemed more than committed to her task.

"You know, you're a complicated woman," he called after her. Intriguing, too, but he wasn't about to tell her that. Would sound too much like a compliment.

"All women are complicated," she called back. "You just never took the time to get to know any of them."

She was, of course, wrong about that. He paid plenty of attention to women. According to her and his mother, that was what had gotten him into trouble in the first place.

"Don't go too far," he called. He would give her enough time, in case she was doing her private business, then go after her.

He wanted to get back to their night shelter and bring some bottles over to the creek. And he wanted to get to higher ground, using the tree cover to see if he could spot the men who were after them. He had to find them, and somehow get ahold of a radio.

The babble of the creek drowned out most sounds around him. He was focused on the bushes she'd disappeared into. Hopefully, she hadn't gotten so mad at him that she'd walked off. He didn't want her to go, even beyond the fact that it was obviously not safe.

He wanted to keep talking with her, getting to know her better. He wanted to know what made her tick, what made her laugh, what made her blue eyes darken with passion. He couldn't remember his mind ever having been this preoccupied with a woman.

Too preoccupied, perhaps.

Because, when the barrel of a gun came to rest against the back of his neck, it caught him unawares.

"Make any noise and I'll blow your head off," a man with an Hispanic accent said. "Get up."

Lazlo got to his feet slowly. He couldn't see his captor, but he could smell the man's stale sweat.

"Now we'll wait for your little friend," the bastard announced.

Not a chance. Lazlo filled his lungs. "Don't come back, Milda. Run!"

Then the man behind him smacked the pistol butt into the back of his head, and the pain shot down his spine, taking all the strength from his legs.

SHE RAN AS FAST as her legs would carry her, until her lungs threatened to collapse. Was someone still following her? She was breathing too hard, the blood rushing in her ears too loudly to hear anything. When she could go no farther, Milda hid under a thick bush, pulling her limbs in, curling up into a ball, hoping to avoid detection if anyone came this way.

Someone *had* come after Lazlo's warning. But it had been a while since she'd heard any branches snap behind her. She lay still, not caring about the bugs or the small lizard that checked her out, stared into her face before turning its shimmering green tail and skittering off.

She was shaking, gasping for air, sweat soaking her skin. *Quiet. Don't make a noise.* Lazlo had been right. She was willing to admit that now. She would have willingly admitted anything, only to be back at home, or at least on the mainland. The island had been a terrible idea. She was never going to do anything like this, ever again.

A bird sang in a tree not far from her. She tried to focus on that instead of all her fears.

After a few interminably long minutes, her racing heart finally slowed. Her breathing was under control. Nobody came. She'd gotten away.

She closed her eyes for a split second, with pure relief, before the next thought hit her. She was alone in the forest. And she had no idea where she was. She'd run forward blindly, changing direction randomly, trying to lose the killer on her trail.

Lazlo would know which way to go. He always did. He seemed to have an innate sense of direction that she'd come to rely on. She relied on him for a number of things, to be fair. Strange for a man whom, for the longest time, she'd believed to be completely unreliable.

He was in the hands of his enemies.

If those men—assassins—she could barely even think the word—hated the royal family as much as he believed they did…

Pain streaked through her chest anew, and it had nothing to do with the way her lungs thirsted for air.

One thought circled her mind, one thought shrunk her stomach into a lead ball, one thought made her eyes burn so much that she had to squeeze them together.

It was entirely possible that they'd already killed him.

Chapter Seven

They had him tied up in Vincent's tent. Lazlo knew this because Ben's had been bloodstained, and this was clean, save for the dirt the three men had tracked in. They were outside at the moment, speaking Spanish, mixing in a lot of English words. Lazlo spoke fluent English, French, German and Italian, but he was unfamiliar with the language they were speaking. Add to that that they were keeping their voices down, and he was lucky to catch every tenth word, not enough to make sense of their conversation.

He still didn't have any idea, beyond guesses, who they were or how they'd gotten to the island. But as fiercely as they protected the place, they planned on leaving at some point. On the way here, he caught sight of a raft in the process of being constructed.

The good news was, they hadn't caught Milda.

The bad news was, they knew she was out there somewhere. And there were three of them. Armed.

He needed to come up with a plan. But even as he tried to loosen his ropes, the one they called Roberto walked into the tent. He'd been able to glean their names as they talked to each other.

"Who are you?" he asked.

Lazlo kept his mouth shut. If these men were with the Freedom Council, they knew exactly who he was.

The man came closer and fingered his clothes, kicked his new hiking boots. His eyes were mean and calculating. "You're a rich man. Give me your money and maybe I'll let you leave the island."

"I have no money." He was speaking the truth. He'd left his wallet in his jacket, which was on the boat that had returned to the mainland.

"Where is your boat?"

"No boat." Maybe the bastards weren't with the Freedom Council, after all. That gave him hope. If the men were after money and not after his life, they might be willing to negotiate.

"How did you get here?" Roberto asked. "You came hunting? Hiking?"

"Hiking. We were dropped off."

"Are you someone important?"

"Hardly."

"You lie," Roberto yelled, and kicked him in the side, this time more viciously.

Pain sliced through Lazlo's ribs. He clenched his jaw tight.

"Your two friends were Valtrian royal security." The man spat, missing Lazlo's head.

"As I am."

Roberto took in his clothes again and the gold watch

on his wrist and gave an evil grin that would have done any silver-screen villain proud. "On closer look, I think you're one of their damn princes."

If he worked for the Freedom Council, he'd know for sure, Lazlo thought. And decided to gamble. "Then negotiate for my release. You have the radios. Make contact."

The man's eyes narrowed suspiciously. He must have been thinking the same thing, but now that Lazlo brought it up, the bastard looked like he was beginning to smell a trap.

Not as stupid as he looked, after all.

"I can't do anything with money if I'm dead. The island would be too easily surrounded." He swore in Spanish, his face twisting into a fierce scowl, as if he blamed Lazlo for everything.

"Let us go then. You have nothing to gain by hurting us. We mean you no harm." He was talking to gain time. After seeing how these men had killed his guards, he had no illusions. The only reason he was still alive was because his apparent wealth and possible status had come as a surprise to Roberto, and it threw the man off temporarily.

The scowl disappeared from the guy's face, replaced by another slow, chilling smile. "Does the name Miguel Santos mean anything to you?"

Lazlo raked his brain. "No. I don't believe so."

Roberto's gaze turned frosty. "It will, before this is all over." He turned and strode out of the tent.

But Lazlo called after him. "Wait. Who is Miguel?"

Roberto stopped and looked back, one hand on the tent flap. "My brother. He was killed in a Valtrian prison. He appealed to the royal family but was denied early release. One of your Valtrian bastards knifed him to death before he could have walked out of there."

The man's chest heaved with emotion, the muscles of his face tight, his gaze burning into Lazlo's. "Before the sun comes up, Miguel will hear your screams in heaven." He spat toward Lazlo, but missed again. "Before the sun comes up, *mi amigo,* you will pray for death."

MILDA SPENT THE REST OF THE DAY under the bush where she'd collapsed, not daring to make any noise by moving, not even after hours had passed, and she was reasonably sure the men had gone. She was scared of everything around her, nearly startled out of her skin when a small animal—a mouse?—skittered across her leg.

But as night fell, she couldn't stop thinking about Lazlo in those killers' clutches. She pushed aside her fears and stole back to the creek, one careful step at a time. Nobody was there, everything was quiet.

She quenched her thirst and ignored her hunger. She couldn't go back to their shelter for food. The Painted Rocks were down the hill, and she needed to go up, in the opposite direction. She felt guilty about the time she'd already wasted.

Going after a group of murderous outlaws seemed insane, but she had to find Lazlo, had to see if she could do anything to help him. She knew she wouldn't be able to fight those men off, but if she could steal a radio while they were busy with Lazlo, at least she could call for help. The chances for dismal failure were astronomical, but she couldn't leave Lazlo to his fate.

She started up the hillside in the cover of the trees, putting one foot in front of the other carefully, stopping frequently to listen. Her pulse went into overdrive every time a piece of fruit fell from a tree. A snake that slithered across her path nearly gave her a heart attack.

At least two hours passed before she reached the top of the hill, the point from where she could see most of the island...and the blinking embers of a small fire in the distance.

There they were, for love's sake. She took a deep breath, relieved that seeking higher ground had been the right decision. Seeing the fire made her feel better about the mess they were in. Lazlo was alive—she felt more sure of that now. He was alive and she would find a way to save him.

She took off immediately, afraid that those embers would cool and she would lose direction. The moon came out from behind the clouds, and the silver light made her trek easier. For the moment, she was grateful for it, even knowing that, once she reached her destination, that light would be nothing but a hindrance, making it easier for the men to spot her approaching.

Another hour passed before she reached them. The

tent was set up next to a car-size rock that shielded it from the sea. That was why they'd been brave enough to light a fire, she realized. No passing boat could see it, especially with the stand of trees behind the rock providing even more thorough covering.

She waited carefully, looking for the slightest movement, listening for the smallest sound. They didn't seem to have a guard waiting. Maybe they thought that, with Lazlo captured, they didn't need one. They probably thought she was holed up somewhere, hiding. Which could work to her advantage.

She approached with as much care as she was capable of. The tent flap stood semiopen. One man slept inside. She couldn't see a radio from her vantage point, and she didn't dare move closer. At least not until she knew where the other one was.

There were two of them, she was pretty sure. She'd heard two when she'd been trapped with Lazlo beneath the rocks at the beach. They must have split up when they captured the prince. One had stayed with him and one had come after her. Thank God, she'd been able to find a good hiding place.

But where was he? And what did they do with their prisoner?

A low moan from the woods brought the answer as she rounded the tent. Her heart raced. She had no plan beyond finding them, but she was too scared to stop and think. And even if she did stop and come up with a plan before going farther, the best plan in the world wouldn't save Lazlo if he was dead by the time she got there.

She crept in the direction of the sound, making sure she was always in cover—not an easy task, as the trees weren't nearly thick enough here to hide her. Then she did see a man at last. Had to be one of the killers. She was so scared she could barely breathe as she watched him. Not stopping to make a plan or find some sort of a weapon seemed insanely stupid all of a sudden. But what experience did she have at something like this? She wasn't a warrior, she was a marital consultant.

The man was alone. Had he been the one to moan? That made little sense. A minute passed before she realized that the odd-shaped tree that held the guy's attention was a tree *and* a man. Her heart practically stopped beating.

Lazlo was tied, with his back against the trunk. His head hung forward and blood dripped from his forehead.

"NOT BAD," Roberto admitted with grudging admiration. He had figured he would have the bastard broken long before now. Many he knew would have already begged for mercy.

He didn't enjoy torture like some of his buddies, but he did it when necessary. He wasn't doing this for his own sake. But if Miguel was watching from above, Roberto wanted his brother to know that he took his death seriously. Where he grew up, women showed their love for a lost one with grief and mourning. A man showed his love for a murdered family member or friend by exacting revenge.

And he was about to kill a prince for Miguel. Brotherly love didn't get greater than that.

He was alone with the prince, not that he knew which one he was—there were four or five of them, he thought. José had gotten tired of the torture and had gone off to sleep. Marco was still out somewhere, looking for the woman.

Roberto drew back the stick he was holding and cracked the man across the shin again, careful not to break the prince's leg. Not yet.

He didn't want the man to go into shock and pass out. He wanted him conscious as long as possible while he beat him to death.

Like his little brother had been beaten and cut in that rat hole of a Valtrian prison. He dropped the stick and pulled the knife he'd gotten off the first man he'd killed on the island. Under other circumstances, he would have figured out a way to make money off the prince. Get the money, then shoot him. But the prince's people would be all over the island if Roberto made contact. And Roberto already had the Italian police after him. The island was too small, with very few places to hide. Bad location, bad timing. At least for a ransom gig. But he would have his revenge, and that in itself was worth something to him.

He had stayed alive this long because he knew the rules. And one of the rules was not to push his luck. Fate had dropped this man into his lap, bringing the revenge he'd so badly wanted right to his doorstep. Hell, the prince might as well have been gift-wrapped.

He planned on taking his sweet time opening this package.

THE VICIOUS CRACK at Lazlo's leg nearly made Milda sick to her stomach. Then the man drew a knife and she felt all the blood leave her head. She blinked a few times and mentally shook herself. She had to act. Now. Or in the next minute, Lazlo would be dead.

She looked for a weapon of any kind, hoping for a heavy, fallen branch. A fist-size stone was the only thing she found. She didn't dare throw it, didn't trust her aim when she had only one chance and her arm was shaking. She inched forward in the cover of the bushes and, when she thought she was close enough, she lunged at the man.

And hit her aim. The stone connected solidly with the back of the bastard's skull. She rolled away immediately, not wanting to get caught if she hadn't succeeded in knocking him out. But she didn't roll fast enough. Rough fingers closed around her ankle and yanked her back.

At least the man had been stunned enough by the blow to drop his knife. Milda saw it on the ground. Out of reach for the both of them.

The man kept her down with a hand splayed in the middle of her chest. She squirmed, but was no match for someone like him. With a roar, he raised the same stone she'd used.

She was a split second from having her skull smashed to pieces. She froze. She always froze when she was scared. She was a lover, not a fighter. She saw the stone come down as if in slow motion.

"Milda," Lazlo called out weakly by the tree.

Hearing his voice gave her strength. She brought her knees up and kicked the man as hard as she could, right where it counted.

The bastard collapsed, then she kicked him in the temple and watched with satisfaction as he fell flat on his back. He stayed on the ground and his eyes rolled back in his head.

She went for his knife and cut Lazlo free. *He was alive*—she hadn't been too late. She wanted to cry with relief. She could have hugged him. She could have kissed him. She held herself back.

He wiped the blood from his face with his sleeve, admiration glinting in his eyes. "You came back." His voice was hoarse, his gaze stunned as he took her in.

"Let's go. The other one is sleeping in the tent." She couldn't be sure if that one hadn't woken up to all the commotion. He could be on them any minute. She didn't have enough strength to fight off another attack, and Lazlo didn't look like he could handle hand-to-hand combat at the moment, either.

He glanced at the motionless figure on the ground, then looked toward the tent. "You go back up the path. I'll take care of that one."

He reached for the knife, and she gave it to him,

relieved to be free of it. "Are you sure? You don't look..."

"He's asleep now. He'll wake up eventually and come after us. We're in no shape to evade him. There's a third one, too. Have you seen him?"

She shook her head. "I'll come with you."

"It'll go faster and easier if I don't have to worry about you stepping into harm's way."

She nodded. Her knees threatened to buckle as she ran up the path, but she kept going. Until she ran into a solid body just around the corner. A young man grabbed her roughly, his face dirty, his thick lips stretching into a mean leer.

"*Puta.* You gave me much work tonight. You better make up for that." He yanked her against him.

His fingers bit into her arms. His breath was bad enough to knock her back. His gaze was emotionless, his eyes endless dark pools, as if there was no soul behind them, nothing whatsoever.

"Lazlo!" she screamed as a shot sounded somewhere behind her.

Then another.

Then Lazlo was running up the path, still bleeding and now breathing hard. He looked like he'd just escaped from hell. She'd never been so happy to see him.

The man shoved her roughly to the ground, pulled his gun and aimed at the prince. But Lazlo got off the first shot and hit his target. The man shouted in pain before he shot back. Then he threw himself into the bushes and ran away.

She remained flat on the ground, her hands over her head, not daring to move, barely daring to breathe.

Lazlo took another shot at the man who was now nothing more than a distant rustling in the bushes, then rushed to her side. "All you all right?"

She nodded, her heart going as fast as if they'd kissed. A nonsensical thought at a time like this.

"You?"

He was beaten and bloodied, but undefeated. He looked larger than life as he extended a hand to her, the kind of hero memorialized in those Valtrian myths on the bookshelves in her room at the palace. "Let's get out of here."

She didn't have to be told twice. She was only too aware that the man who'd grabbed her was still armed, still out there somewhere in the darkness.

HOURS HAD PASSED since they'd arrived back at the Painted Rocks, but Lazlo was still frustrated on every possible level.

He hadn't been able to protect Milda. That bothered him the most. He'd been captured. She could have been killed.

He hadn't been able to take out all three of the bastards. He didn't know for sure if Milda had gotten Roberto for good. He'd taken out José and was on his way back to his torturer when Milda had screamed and he'd rushed to her instead. He wasn't sure if his second bullet found Marco, either. Or whether the first one had caused enough damage to kill him eventually.

And without knowing that, he didn't want to leave Milda alone to go back and finish Roberto. Nor did it seem safe to take her with him since Roberto might have recovered enough to arm himself in the meanwhile.

Milda sat quietly, staring into the night.

She had saved him.

She had put her life on the line to rescue him. He didn't see that coming. He would have expected that from his guards and from his brothers, but not from a matchmaker he'd been less than civil to on a number of occasions.

She truly was one of a kind, the most extraordinary woman he'd ever met. She played no games. She asked for no gifts, accepted no bribes. She was honest, sometimes painfully so. Levelheaded. Brave. And she was beautiful, too. He couldn't understand why he'd ever thought her crooked lips less than the most tempting sight he'd ever seen.

"So how come a marital consultant like you isn't married? Wouldn't that be the best advertisement?" he asked, even as he found himself oddly annoyed at the thought of her with another man.

They were back in the crevice at Painted Rocks. They'd eaten more of their food. She had more smoked salmon. He had canned soup. She'd taken care of his wounds, disinfected them with champagne—reasoning that alcohol was alcohol. They only had a few hours to go until dawn. They should be resting, but they were both too wired to sleep.

The moon bathed her face, including her raised eyebrows, in a silver glow. "Marital consultant?"

He'd forgotten to tease her with the matchmaker thing. "Forget the things I said before," he told her. "You have my full respect."

The eyebrows went down. The pleased expression that appeared on her face made her look even more breathtaking.

"I've dated…." She hesitated as she answered his question. "Most of the time when I meet a guy, the first thing I think of is whether he'd be right for any of my clients."

"The cobbler who has holes in his shoes?"

She nodded.

"I can't imagine men not pursuing you," he observed, again, the thought uncomfortable. He didn't want to think of another man within a mile of her. She was too earnest, too honest, too well meaning. Someone could take advantage of her. It wasn't that he was interested in her personally, he told himself, but he didn't want to see her hurt.

"If they do, it ends pretty fast." She turned away, looking out at the sea. "They tend not to be crazy about my occupation. They're afraid that I know all the tricks of the trade to trap them."

He couldn't say much to that. He'd entertained the same thoughts when they'd first met. He'd avoided her every chance he got. What a fool he'd been, he thought. Five whole months wasted.

But then, did that mean that he *was* interested in her personally?

Only one way to find out.

He drew her into her arms slowly, gently, giving her time.

She didn't pull away. "How are you feeling?" she asked, snuggling closer to him.

And he felt a sense of peace that he'd never felt with a woman before. "Sore everywhere." But not too sore to do something about it if she turned in his arms.

She didn't. "At least I got there before he was able to use the knife."

"And for that, you have my undying gratitude." He meant that. He would never forget the way she had appeared out of the night, scared stiff, to save him.

"Tomorrow we'll go back to the stream, wash your wounds with clean water and rebandage them."

"Good. I don't think I can handle another champagne treatment." The alcohol might have been good for disinfecting, but it stung like hell. While she'd bandaged him in strips of his pants leg, he ended up finishing the bottle.

He must have looked like a mummy in raggedy shorts. He presented a less dashing picture than he was used to. But Milda had just smiled at him. And he found that, as long as she found it entertaining, he didn't mind being disheveled.

Peace surrounded them. He was almost certain that

they would be safe for the night. Roberto and Marco, if they were alive, would need time to regroup. One or both were seriously wounded. They wouldn't mount a manhunt in the middle of the night.

Gradually, the pain in his body abated, other sensations taking its place. To go with them or not, that was the question. To hell with hesitation, he thought then. He knew what he wanted with sudden clarity, and he'd just escaped death's jaw. Not that he'd ever been afraid of taking chances.

He reached up to caress Milda's arm, gliding his fingertip softly along her smooth skin, his touch barely a whisper. He didn't want to give her a reason to protest. She lay with her back to him. He pressed his lips behind her ear. Then down her neck, paying special attention to the heart-shaped mole there.

She was so incredibly soft everywhere. He wanted to investigate every inch of her body. His blood heated as it pumped through his veins. His fingers found their way over to the firm swell of her breast. His body hardened, predictably, and he kissed her neck again. His thumb found her nipple, a hard little knob that right now seemed the most fascinating thing in the universe.

So she wasn't completely unaffected by him.

He hated the obstruction of clothes between them.

His hand slid down to the button on her pants. He could already see them both naked, pressed together. He could no longer feel any pain. All he could feel was her incredible body against his. All he could think of was sliding into her tight heat, taking her.

He tugged her shirt loose. Then he splayed his fingers across her flat stomach, touching smooth skin again. He wanted to press his lips there. Not yet. But soon. For now, he went as slowly as he possibly could. He wanted to show her how good this could be between them.

He wanted her to feel. His hand moved up, his fingers reaching her bra. Lacy. Normally, he appreciated frills like that. But right now he resented any impediment. Still, he bade himself to be patient, and outlined the lace edging with his fingers.

A soft shiver ran through her, even as she put her hand over his to still it. "Shouldn't you rest?" Her voice was heavy, but not with sleep.

The sound shot even more desire through his body.

Rest? Not with her pressed against him. "I can't."

"And I can't do this," she said, but her voice was full of uncertainty, which gave him hope. "You're a client."

"The Queen hired you, not me."

She turned at last, but only to look into his eyes, not to throw herself into his arms. "We agreed that this wasn't going to happen."

"Because it would break some unwritten rule for you?" He reached a new level of frustration all of a sudden.

"Among other things."

"You could always quit and find another line of work."

She pulled back. There was that wall again. "What else would I be?" she asked, exasperated.

"A teacher. An actress...a princess," he added, before he could stop himself.

He'd never said that to any woman. Never thought he would, had always studiously avoided making any false promises.

For a moment, time stood still.

Then she shook her head. "Don't do this. You're a born seducer. You can't help yourself." She pulled back, out of his arms. "Look, you're very attractive. It's...it's not fair."

He didn't want to be fair. "Why couldn't it work? What do you have against me?"

"Are you kidding?" She gave a sour laugh. "You chase after anything in a skirt. You have no idea how to care about a woman, how to be faithful, how to love."

That stung. She was being incredibly unfair.

"I love my mother, I love my brothers and I love my country." And he knew how to care, too. He cared about his people, his employees at the factory. *About her.* Earlier, when she'd come to his rescue, he had spotted her in the bushes. And willed her to go away. He would have rather faced more of Roberto's torture than have something happen to her. His heart had nearly stopped when she'd lunged forward to stop Roberto.

The relief of having her back here with him, safe, was indescribable. Every cell inside him insisted on celebrating life in the most basic way possible.

"I care about a lot of things," he assured her.

"That's not the same, and you know it. With all due

respect, you have no idea how to be in a meaningful relationship."

Did he want to be in a meaningful relationship? He hadn't before. But with her... He didn't think he could tire of Milda anytime soon. Maybe never.

"Teach me then." He reached for her. "You're the expert."

She wouldn't move closer. She was visibly pulling herself together. The passion was gone from her voice when she said, "I came here to do a job, not to have my heart broken."

"I see." She was deliberately misunderstanding him. Again. He let it go, not wanting to push her. But he wasn't giving up. He was a prince. He wasn't easily thwarted.

Chapter Eight

Milda woke to an uncomfortable feeling in her stomach.

Alone.

Again.

Last night... She sat up when she remembered that she'd nearly given in to the prince. For a moment there she believed him, believed that he could be seriously interested in someone like her for a change. For love's sake, she couldn't be that foolish. She wouldn't.

She knew him. She knew how he was. He could never take a woman seriously, beyond a quick affair. Sure, that would have been fun. He was wonderfully male, had the greatest body she'd ever had the good luck to snuggle against—eyes and voice made for seduction. When he touched her, when he kissed her...her body responded to him fully. He would be a wonderful lover.

But she craved more. And less, in some ways. She wanted someone ordinary and simple. She wanted forever. She wanted a family. A family to replace the one she had lost, not that they could ever be replaced completely.

The part she loved most about her job was that she was creating families. That gave her a sense of satisfaction that nothing else could. It helped her forget, even if only temporarily, that she didn't have a family of her own. Being invited to those weddings and christenings mattered so much because there she could pretend that she was part of some unit and not all alone in the world.

A brief fling with Lazlo wouldn't solve anything. She had more self-respect than to allow herself to become another notch on the prince's bedpost—even if she was more attracted to him than to any other man she'd ever met. That would pass. She could ignore whatever insanity drew her to him. She was a professional.

She ran her fingers through her hair, then went to relieve herself in the bushes. A slight cramp ran through her stomach as she straightened. She pressed her hand against the pain. Here was the result of drinking champagne instead of water, and eating erratically.

She spotted Lazlo on her way back. He sat where he could see most of the area above and below them. She went to sit next to him.

"So, leaving before the woman you slept with wakes up is an ingrained habit with you, is it?" she asked, to remind herself what a colossally bad idea it would be to fall for him. A reminder she needed.

He looked at her, the rising sun behind him. His gaze took in her face, not missing any detail.

And she regretted her sharp remark. Her attraction to him wasn't his fault. She should be annoyed with herself, not with him.

"Maybe I don't trust myself around you in the mornings," he said quietly.

She felt her face heat.

"We need to go back to the creek and get some water today," he said, changing the subject suddenly, turning back to his survey of the island.

"What if the men go for water?"

"It's a chance we have to take."

He was right. They weren't drinking nearly enough, not even with the champagne. And maybe some cold, clear water would settle her stomach.

"Maybe those men are dead," she said, knowing she was probably being too optimistic. But it could have happened. Lazlo said he'd taken out the one in the tent. She'd hit and kicked the one who had tortured him as hard as she'd been able. And Lazlo had shot the young guy who'd run into the woods once for sure.

"That would be nice. But we shouldn't count on it." He stood and offered her his hand.

She accepted the help, acknowledged the electric current that passed between them and prudently let him go the second she was standing.

"How about breakfast before we head out?" he asked.

"Not hungry right now. Maybe when we come back. But you should eat. Go ahead."

"I'd rather go for water first, too. Before it gets too hot out here."

They walked back to the crevice together.

She'd had some practice at averting her eyes from the painted images, and did that now, as soon as they came into view. "I still wouldn't mind moving someplace else."

"The crevice is protected on two sides, and you can't see it until you're nearly upon it. We haven't been found so far. We should stick to what works." He dumped out the remaining food from the duffel bag, then placed the two empty champagne bottles and two empty cans inside.

She stumbled after him as he started out. She needed caffeine badly. Maybe her stomach problem was a withdrawal symptom. At home, the first thing she did each morning was drink a cup of coffee. She couldn't get dressed without it.

She might have given a little moan, because he asked, "What's wrong?" in a whisper, looking alert, looking her over.

"Just thinking."

He relaxed. "About what?"

"Everyone who complains about their job in an air-conditioned office, with the coffeepot around the corner, should try being a castaway for a week."

"You have an office?" He resumed walking.

That this would surprise him annoyed her. "I *am* a professional."

"Didn't mean it as an offense. All I meant was that

you're one person. No employees. You could work out of your house. Isn't that what everyone wants? To go to work in their pajamas?"

"Is that what you want?" She resisted picturing him in pajamas. Especially since her gut feeling said he was the type who would definitely sleep in the buff.

"I want to work, play and sleep at the racetrack," he confessed, with a disarming smile that she was beginning to like too much.

So she focused on something else instead. "I don't want to receive clients in my apartment." Aside from the privacy issue, they might lose confidence in her if they realized how modestly she lived. Her apartment didn't exactly portray an image of success. Her income was way down in the last couple of years.

"I do what they call 'office sharing.'" To keep costs down.

"With a divorce attorney?" he teased. "Get them coming and going?"

"You're hilarious." She made a face at him. "Lawyers can afford their own offices. I share with a psychic."

He made no comment, but she could tell from the expression on his face that it strained him.

"So, what's the most difficult part of your job?" he asked after a while, moving forward quietly, keeping his voice down, only turning to look at her now and then.

You, she wanted to say. But since she wasn't feeling up to par this morning, she decided it would be better not to start an argument with him. "Clients who know exactly what they need."

He did glance back at that. "How is that wrong?"

"They'll ask for someone who is professional, financially established, a certain religion. Then I find someone just like that and the client goes along for a while before he or she realizes that their date doesn't make their heart sing."

He sounded thoughtful as he said, "A person to make your heart sing?"

She nodded, even though he couldn't see her. "Exactly. You'll meet her one day. Soon, I hope," she added. And then, because the thought twisted something deep inside her chest, she added a snide remark. "You certainly seem to meet enough women."

He stopped and turned around to face her. "You do know that I don't bed every woman I meet?"

"Could have fooled me. How about the ladies who left us here?"

"I said I dated them. There might have been a couple of dinner invitations."

"As far as you remember."

"Fine, as far as I remember. I'm a sociable person. I like to go out. I like beautiful women." He paused. "Did they say that we—"

Her cheeks burned. Which was so insane. *He* should have been embarrassed. "I didn't ask intimate questions."

They fell quiet for the last leg of their trek, mindful that the men might be headed for the water, too. When she finally heard the creek—and then saw it—she realized Lazlo had picked a different spot, a little farther down the hillside.

The water felt incredible. She couldn't stop drinking. He rinsed the bottles. She rinsed the cans. Then they filled them.

"I'll hand-carry the cans so they don't spill. You can bring the bottles in the bag," he told her in a whisper, keeping his eyes on the surrounding vegetation. He was ready to go.

"Could I take a quick dip, you think?" The creek wasn't nearly deep enough to swim in, but she could sit in the water, or even lay in it. She'd sweated through her shirt on the way here. Feeling clean would have been nice. And the cold water might make her feel a little better. The sun was already high enough in the sky so that her clothes would dry in minutes.

He hesitated, but then he said, "All right. Try not to make any noise. You have two minutes."

He kept lookout while she bathed. Since she kept her clothes on, there was no reason to feel shy in front of him, but she did.

"You could turn around."

"I want to monitor both sides of the creek."

He was only a few steps away, the situation oddly intimate. He kept his eyes on their surroundings for the most part. But from time to time, his dark gaze did stray to her.

She splashed water into her face. On her neck. Oh, the hell with it, she thought then and lay right down, letting the water trickle over her, keeping only her face out so she could breathe. "I can't imagine anything more refreshing," she said as the dust and sweat of their long walk washed away.

He said nothing.

"Your turn." She submerged completely before she stood, nearly slipping, then walked out, keeping her arms crossed in front of her breasts.

He set the cans down and avoided looking at her. "We can probably spare another minute."

THIS TIME SHE STOOD sentinel and kept scanning the bushes, aware that any of them could hide an attacker. She studiously avoided looking at Lazlo. Managed for two whole minutes.

He didn't leave his clothes on.

He squatted, wearing his black shorts, in the deepest part of the water, which was only eight or nine inches deep at that spot. He was throwing water on his head, wetting his hair. Water ran down his impressive back in rivulets, dappled sunlight making the scene seem like an artistic photograph.

But not the kind he collected—antique photos of the first automobiles. This picture could have been in a wall calendar made for women. Even his scars looked artistic from this angle.

A deep yearning rose inside her, an elemental need she hadn't known was there. Her throat went dry as she watched him. Every movement showed the strength of the man. He was alert, unhurried, keeping his gaze on the opposite bank.

Then he turned.

And caught her watching him.

The expression on his face changed, heat coming into his gaze. He stood slowly, his tanned skin glistening. He took a step toward her. Then another.

A wave of dizziness washed over her. The next second, a cramp in her stomach made her double over. Then he was there.

"What's wrong?"

"I think I'm getting dehydrated."

"What hurts?"

"My stomach."

He helped her sit.

"I'm fine. It already passed." She glanced up at him, aware of his lack of clothing, of his hands on her shoulders.

"Let's get back to the Painted Rocks." He dressed hurriedly, then picked up their bag and the cans. "Stay behind me."

"I'm fine. Could be the sun." They'd spent too much time outside in the past couple of days.

He looked grim, as if not buying her explanation. "Did it just start hurting?"

"I had a few twinges yesterday."

He scowled. "Why didn't you say something?"

"We've been living on champagne, caviar and wild fruit. I thought my body was just adjusting to the circumstances."

Another cramp came, this one stronger, stealing her breath away. She felt the blood run out of her face and her knees weaken. She leaned against a tree. She was dizzy again.

He handed her the cans and picked her up. Suddenly, she was too weak to protest. "My ears are ringing."

By the time he got them back to their shelter, half the water had sloshed from the cans, but she was feeling better again—and foolish for having made such a fuss over what was most likely nothing. "I'll be fine in a couple of hours. Don't worry about it."

"As soon as night falls, I'm going back to the men. We need that radio. You're sick. You need medical help." He paced. "I think they're building a raft. I saw something in a clearing near the shore when Roberto was marching me back to their tent. We could steal that and get off the island."

"No," she said immediately.

"If we can't get the radio, that might be our only chance."

"The mainland is too far away. Maybe they can risk their lives like that, but you can't. You're a prince."

He poured the remaining water from the smaller can to fill up the bigger one, then sat on a rock and began hammering the empty can with a fist-size stone he'd wrapped in a piece of his shirt to muffle the sound. His mouth pulled tight as he looked out over the side of the hill. "I'll take my chances."

"I won't. I'm a terrible swimmer."

He only hesitated a second before he said, "It has to be the radio then."

"I'll be better by tonight, and we'll go get it together in the morning."

"I won't allow that."

Oh, please, she thought, but before she could object to his imperial style, a wave of nausea rolled over her. She got up, started toward the bushes. Lazlo stood to go with her.

"I need a moment of privacy."

"What if you fall?"

"Please." She didn't want to throw up in front of the prince.

He seemed to understand, but didn't look like he liked it. "Call if you need me."

She kept plodding forward. Then went a little farther. She didn't want him to hear her give back her last meal.

Another roll of nausea came. She squeezed her eyes shut. She was rarely sick. Catching some bug out here where she couldn't get any help was so unfair. If she got sick, she was going to hold Lazlo back. And she would be no help whatsoever if the men found them.

She braced an arm on the trunk of an old olive tree. A soft noise came from the bushes behind her. She didn't turn. "I'll be fine. Please go back."

But the prince didn't respond. Instead, she was grabbed roughly by the neck. She smelled unwashed, sweaty male. Opened her mouth to scream. But a large, dirty palm cut off her air.

She fought against the man who was dragging her away from Painted Rocks, fought as hard as she could until the next stomach cramp came and she lost all her strength for a minute.

Then she heaved.

The man swore in another language and snatched his hand from her mouth, but didn't let her go. Which meant that she ended up throwing up all over him.

Oh, God, that felt so much better. But he wouldn't let her sink to the ground. He slapped her across the face, then dragged her along as if nothing had happened.

He dragged her by the arm now, bruising her. She kicked out, too dizzy to put up a real fight. A murderous madman had her, and she could do little about it. Lazlo wouldn't even notice that she was gone until it was too late. And to be honest, part of her was glad about that. That way, at least the prince couldn't come after her, wouldn't come to harm.

She felt responsible for how things had turned out. She was the one who had tricked him into coming to the island.

Her stomach hurt and her head swam as the man dragged her along. When she realized that no amount of scratching and kicking would free her, she began grabbing for the branches they passed. But when she got a firm grip on one, it barely slowed the man's progress. He yanked her violently, nearly ripping her arm from the socket, and she was forced to let go.

She expected him to take her back to the campsite where she'd found Lazlo, but the man was carrying her up the hillside in another direction. This was the slope where they'd found the second guard's body in the woods.

Think, think, think. Not an easy task when her stomach was heaving and her head spinning.

She'd been gone for at least fifteen minutes now. Lazlo would start looking. She desperately wanted him to find her, but she wanted him to stay safe just as badly.

She had to save herself.

She refused to die here.

She was weak, thanks to her stomach, but the man was tiring, too. She dragged her feet, putting up as much resistance as possible, to exhaust him sooner. By the time they reached the clearing, his grip was loosening.

The well she'd fallen into was somewhere up ahead. Which gave her an idea.

She gave a loud moan, then made as if collapsing, heaved. The man let her drop to the ground this time, taking a quick step back. She rolled away from him as soon as she hit the ground. Then she was on her feet and running.

"You stupid—" The rest came out in his native language.

He was right behind her.

Her first burst of energy ran out quicker than she had anticipated. The nausea and dizziness weren't helping. If she could make it to the well… She gave everything she had.

The tip of his fingers touched her back, but it was too late. She jumped.

He went down the hole, shouting.

She collapsed on the other side, her knees wobbly, her lungs burning. She did her best to catch her breath. Almost succeeded, before she threw up again. When she was done, she rolled onto her back and stared up at the sky. God, she hated feeling sick. But at least she was safe for the moment.

Only a moment, she realized, as a noise drew her attention to the well. Rocks scraped under the man's shoes as he fought his way up, and she remembered that Lazlo had been able to get out of there without much trouble.

No time to rest now. She pushed to her feet, her limbs dangerously weak. But she didn't get farther than a few yards before the man shouted behind her. His head and arms were above the rim of the well. He was holding his gun on her.

How could she forget about the weapon? It must have been under his shirt all along. But he hadn't thought it was necessary to use until now. He'd thought taking her would be easy. And he'd probably wanted her alive. Now, with his head bleeding, he looked mad enough not to care anymore.

She froze as he pulled his body up and climbed out. This was it. The end.

But then Lazlo stole out of the woods behind the man, carrying a long, straight branch. She kept her eyes on her attacker, praying that he wouldn't turn. Of course, he did. And immediately took aim at Lazlo.

But Lazlo had already launched his makeshift spear. The sharp end went through the man's throat, and he fell to the ground, dropping the gun, clutching at the spurting blood, writhing.

She staggered toward Lazlo as he ran to her. "Where did you get that?"

"Made a tip from that can we weren't using." He pushed her behind him and walked toward the man carefully, grabbed the gun, then searched the man's pockets. "No radio. He must have passed it on to José."

"Finish him." She wanted to make sure the bastard was dead, that he could never come after her and Lazlo again.

"He's finished," he said simply, taking her hand. "And I might need all the bullets we have to keep us safe. Or to signal for help," he added, then paused for a second, as with a mighty groan, the man pulled himself to his knees.

He gripped the spear's handle with both hands, his eyes bulging. He was trying to remove the spear, but ended up lurching back instead. Into the well. Then everything went quiet.

Lazlo went to the well, holding the gun in front of him. He looked down. "Broke his neck," he said as he turned to her.

She looked away. The man had come to a gruesome end, but she couldn't feel sorry for him. Not when she remembered the two royal guards who'd been killed in cold blood. The man in the bottom of the well had gotten what he deserved.

Lazlo drew her forward. They didn't stop until they were in the woods, in the cover of the trees. Then he looked her over. "Did he hurt you?"

"He didn't have a chance. I fought him all the way."

The tight lines of his face relaxed. "How are you feeling?"

"Okay."

He tucked his gun away and picked her up without warning, carried her back to their crevice.

The closer they got, the worse she felt. By the time he gently placed her on their blanket, her head was swimming again. "Face it, Gilligan, you're never getting off this island," she muttered miserably, regretting that she'd ever set foot here.

Lazlo stilled. "Who is Gilligan?"

Of course he wouldn't get the cultural reference. Valtrian TV stations ran Valtrian shows. Although she'd seen some syndicated prime-time dramas since she'd been in the country, they tended to be the latest U.S. and U.K. top hits. He'd probably never seen a single rerun of *Gilligan's Island.* And she didn't have the energy to explain.

"An ex-boyfriend?" He frowned.

"A fictional character."

"Forget him. I'll get you back to the mainland. I promise you that."

The thing was, she believed him. She just hoped it wouldn't be too late.

He watched her for a few seconds, then moved to their food stock and began sorting it into four piles, carefully checking the cans and all the packaging. His movements were deliberate, unhurried, his focus on his task. Only the tight set of his jaw betrayed that he was fighting some emotion.

"What are you doing?" She hoped he wasn't going to eat. She was afraid the smell and sight of food would push her over the edge again. She needed a break. She was sure that if she could just rest for a few minutes, she would feel much better.

"This is what neither of us ate from." He pointed at the first pile. "This is what we both ate from. This is what only I ate from. And this—" his mouth tightened as he indicated the last pile "—is what only you ate."

The last thing she wanted to talk about was food. But something in his face made her ask, "And?"

He watched her as if weighing whether or not to say more. But then he drew a slow breath and held her gaze. "I think you've been poisoned."

Chapter Nine

When someone was dehydrated enough to have symptoms this severe, other signs showed as well, but Milda's eyes weren't sunk in, her skin felt elastic and supple. He checked.

His thoughts kept coming back to the smoked salmon that she'd eaten. Since she liked it so much, he'd left it all for her.

He made her drink as much water as she could keep down, hoping it would flush her system. By the time night fell again, she seemed to be resting more comfortably. He wasn't. Dark rage coursed through him. If anything happened to her, there'd be hell to pay. He could and would find the bastard who was responsible for this.

"Are you still hurting?" Lazlo asked, as calmly as he was capable, not wanting to let on just how precarious her situation was.

"The stomach cramps have passed." She looked pale in the moonlight.

Cooler night air came from the sea. "Do you want

me to light a fire?" Only, Roberto could still be alive. If the bastard *was* alive, and the light of the fire led him here, Lazlo would deal with him.

"No fire. It's too hot already."

Except it wasn't. He moved closer and placed a hand on her forehead. Worry tightened the muscles of his jaw. "You're running a fever."

She gave a resigned groan. "Figures." She closed her eyes. "I can't believe the food spoiled. The bag had been in the ocean, in cold water. That's as good as a refrigerator, isn't it? And everything was canned or shrink-wrapped. How could I get food poisoning from that?"

"Not food poisoning. Someone did this. On purpose." And now she had a fever. He had to do something about that.

"But these men had no access to our food." She opened her eyes and gave him a look of confusion.

"Not these men. The Freedom Council."

She fell silent. Then, after a moment she said, "That can't be. The food was prepared in the royal kitchen. No outsiders have access to it, do they?"

"They don't." The royal kitchen had top-notch security. And yet, it had somehow been infiltrated. "The Freedom Council thought, like I did, that the six princes would be coming to the island. They found a way to get to the food. The temptation was too much, I suppose."

"You mean, like the cook, or someone on his team, betrayed you?"

"Or someone who had access to the food during transportation. Between the kitchen staff and those who have access to the kitchen and transport, at least two dozen people could have found a moment to tamper with the packages." He remembered a discussion he'd had with his brothers a while back. "Benedek was right," he said under his breath. Of course, his twin brother often was.

"About what?"

"When he was in the catacombs with Rayne after the attack on the opera house, he heard a group of rebels down there. And one of the voices was familiar to him. He couldn't place it, but he swore that he'd heard that man speak before. He insisted that the enemy had someone inside the castle." He paused to think over the implications. "I didn't believe him."

"And now?"

"We need to get off this island and warn my family. I'm going to catch this bastard."

"Just be careful," she said weakly.

He watched her for a moment. Then he picked up the gun that was sitting on the rock beside him and handed it to her. "Hang on to this. If Roberto comes by, shoot him the second you spot him."

Her eyes went wide. "And you?"

"I'm going back to the creek." He gathered up all their empty containers in the canvas bag. "I'll be back as fast as I can."

"Please don't leave," she pleaded, pulling up to a sitting position.

He hesitated only for a second. Her fever had to be dealt with. "If I hear a shot, I'll come flying." Then he strode into the woods before he could change his mind.

That the Freedom Council had found a way, yet again, to get to the royal family didn't even surprise him anymore. They had money, which meant power. They were bound to find a way. He was a royal prince. He knew the risks. But Milda coming to harm…

Anger clenched his muscles tighter as he strode forward in the night. The need to stay quiet tempered his need for speed. The woods were considerably darker than the sparse area around their crevice, the branches above blocking out moonlight for the most part.

It didn't take long before he lost his points of reference. He stopped to regain his bearings, and realized that the unfamiliar feeling that was tearing him apart was despair. Except that he didn't despair. He was the easygoing prince.

But at some point Milda had become important to him. He cared more than he wanted to admit, about this pesky matchmaker—marital consultant, he corrected himself—holed up in a small crevice somewhere behind him, possibly dying.

Because of him.

And it was as if part of him was dying just thinking about that. Over the past couple of insane days, Milda Milas had come to *mean* something to him. She'd gained his trust and admiration, she'd become a friend—a sort of reluctant partner in survival.

It was a new experience for him, a relationship that he found he was desperate to keep. Even if the very word "relationship" scared him more than being stuck on the island with a cold-blooded killer who wanted to see him dead. Self-preservation dictated that he keep his thoughts on his enemy and on figuring out a way to defeat the man. But his mind wanted to dwell on Milda. As if somehow, in the middle of all the craziness, she had become the most important—

The thought stilled him. And in that moment of silence, he heard the distant call of the creek.

Ten minutes passed before he reached it. Then another forty minutes by the time he got back to Milda, careful again not to make too much noise, in case Roberto was out there hunting for them; careful, also, not to spill any water.

She was sitting with her back against the rock, the gun aimed at him as he stepped out of the bushes.

"It's me."

She lowered the weapon.

He noticed the small tremble in her arm. She looked weak, but she was still able to sit upright. That was something. "Feeling any better?" He searched her face.

She lay down on the folded-up tent, as if only nerves had kept her together while he'd been gone. "About the same." Her slim fingers worried the colorful bracelet on her left wrist.

"What's that made of, anyway?" he asked, to distract himself from how concerned he was about her.

"Love beads," she said sheepishly.

He resisted rolling his eyes. The woman took the whole love thing too far. He simply said, "Interesting," then lined up the water-filled champagne bottles and cans on the rock beside her. When he was done, he stepped back and used a sharp piece of metal that he'd scrapped when he'd put together his makeshift spear, and used it to slice off his other pant leg. His once elegant pants were now frayed shorts.

"If *Time* magazine could see me now," he muttered, with irony in his voice. They'd done a piece on him the year before, entitled: "Gentleman, Businessman, Prince." His normally impeccable style merited five whole paragraphs. As opposed to the single sentence about his charities toward the end of the article, the reason why he'd agreed to the interview in the first place.

They'd simply used him to sell more copies. Out of a hundred people he met, ninety-nine wondered how he could be of use to them. Yet another way his title trapped him.

Milda was giving him a weak smile. "You're beginning to look like a real castaway." She watched as he dipped the cloth into the largest water can, the one that at one time had held some incredibly delicious Valtrian peaches. "What are you doing?"

"I'm going to wash you off in some cool water. We need to bring down your fever."

He washed her face first, carefully, feeling the heat radiating off her. She closed her eyes, but it took little imagination to conjure up her familiar, knowing, lively gaze. Nothing was lively about her now. He hated the listlessness that took possession of her.

"You'll be fine. We'll get off this island. I promise."

She didn't say anything in response.

He dunked the cloth into the can, then squeezed out the excess water. He washed her face again, then her neck, as far as her shirt allowed. Not too far. She wasn't into plunging necklines.

He found now, to his surprise, that he liked that about her. She had an amazing body—he'd seen that every time her clothes got wet—but she didn't feel the need to put her assets on display every minute of every day. That spoke of self-assurance and the kind of sense of security that the models and actresses he'd dated rarely possessed.

She was different from most women he knew; he'd known that from the beginning, when he had come on to her. Her response had definitely not been the usual, what he'd come to expect.

They'd been in his office. She was working through an endless list of questions about him—his personality, what attracted him, and so on. He was nothing but a client to her. She was completely unaware of him as a man. And she was dead set on putting an end to his freedom. Which had seriously annoyed him.

So he strode up to her to take a look at the notes she was writing in her little personal organizer thing, thinking that he hadn't seen a paper one of those in years. She clearly hadn't yet moved into the twenty-first century. She'd worn a prim suit, her hair pulled away from her face. He'd leaned forward to see what she was writing.

And caught the scent of vanilla.

Nobody wore vanilla perfume. Absolutely nobody. Maybe young schoolgirls. He'd tried to discern what that told him about her, trying to pin down the enemy. But while he was thinking hard about his next move, that plain, faint vanilla scent had somehow gotten to him.

As did the soft strands of her hair, curled against her slim neck, hair that had clearly never seen artificial coloring. Her cheeks were not covered by foundation. And he'd marveled at her luminous skin.

The crook of her neck, the only bare spot exposed on her body, was inches from his lips. He wanted to kiss the heart-shaped mole there, even if he was certain that it was fake. She took the whole matchmaker/ambassador of love thing too far.

Not his type, some sane part of his mind had said.

But the rest of him hadn't cared.

She's going to be trouble. One last, reasonable thought surfaced.

But all he could think of was, *Well, if she's going to be trouble anyway...*

And then he'd leaned forward and kissed her soft skin. The heart-shaped mole was real.

She'd jumped out of her chair and was on the

other side of the table before he could blink. "Your Highness!"

"We could skip all the hard work and see if we might find a more pleasant way to pass the afternoon," he'd suggested.

She had succeeded in thoroughly distracting him. He'd thought maybe he could turn the tables on her and distract her from marrying him off to some woman of her choosing.

Women frequently developed passionate and mostly unrequited attachments to him. If she did, maybe she wouldn't push for some nightmare of a marriage with an "appropriate" lady. The idea had seemed brilliant. A lover who drew him for reasons he couldn't explain, and a way to gain safety.

But she had expressed, in the most polite—not to mention firm—terms, that she could never, under any circumstances—

"That feels nice." Her words cut off his memories.

Just as well. They were on the embarrassing side. He hadn't experienced much rejection as a prince. After that incident, they were firmly on opposing sides. She'd made it clear that she would do anything to see him married. He was equally determined to avoid that fate. He couldn't imagine coming home to the same person every night. *Having* to come home every night. Probably at the same time, or the wife would be upset that dinner had gotten cold, or that he left their guests waiting or whatever. Royal protocol already took up an inordinate amount of his time, time he would have rather spent on his cars and business.

Except, he'd barely thought about his cars and business since he'd been on the island with Milda. She had a way of filling out his time most interestingly, a way of invading his thoughts. And for some strange reason, he didn't even mind it.

Desert Island Syndrome, he reminded himself, then moistened and squeezed the cloth again, and after folding it, placed it on her forehead, leaving it there this time.

They sat quietly for the next few minutes. Then he reached for the cloth to change it again. Her forehead hadn't cooled enough. If anything, it was even hotter than before he'd started. His cure wasn't working.

He glanced at the bottles and cans of water, then at her. "I'm going to have to remove your clothes." He paused when her eyes went wide. "I'm sorry. It's a medical necessity."

"I bet you say that to all the women." She smiled weakly, but sat and pulled off her shirt and pants herself.

Moonlight gilded a body that would have thoroughly seduced him under different circumstances.

He busied himself by pouring out all the water they had, save one bottle, and soaking their only blanket. "Here." He lifted her up and wrapped her in the wet, soggy fabric.

In a minute, her teeth were chattering. "I'm freezing."

"You can put your dry clothes back on as soon as

your temperature comes down a little." He hated that he could do nothing for her beyond this. Or maybe one more thing. He lifted the bottle to her lips. "Drink."

"You're very bossy," she said before she did as he'd asked.

He shrugged. "Comes with the territory."

"Along with an endless supply of beautiful women?" she asked when she was done drinking. "You must be going through withdrawal by now."

He should be. He never lacked female company. But being on the island with Milda wasn't altogether bad. He had a feeling that, under different circumstances, they might have enjoyed their two secluded weeks. There were a couple of Etruscan ruins he remembered from his childhood that he wouldn't have minded showing her.

She tended to be amazed by anything older than a couple of hundred years—older than the U.S., her home country. She was forever admiring the palace and its artifacts. In fact, that had been one of the few things he'd been able to use now and then to successfully distract her from her matchmaking. Not nearly enough, but it had been something. He was grateful for even the smallest reprieve.

"You can catch up when we get back to the palace."

A moment passed by the time he realized she was still talking about women.

"I've cut back lately, actually."

She managed a weak snort.

But he was speaking the truth. He'd gone out less, and he kept his socializing to clubs and restaurants, going home afterwards. For the last couple of months, at least.

Maybe he was getting old.

Or maybe, with Milda trying to hook him up left and right with the most suitable women, he needed a break.

"Maybe I'm in a slump." He'd heard others talk about that before, but back then he hadn't fully understood what that meant.

Milda rolled her eyes. "I'm sure you'll recover."

He wasn't worried. They would get off this island; her assignment would be up. She would stop pestering him with her matchmaking. His strange new attraction to her would no doubt clear up as well, once he was back at court among all those ladies. Their friendship, or whatever it was that had grown between them, would fizzle out. She'd go back home to her life and he'd go back to his. Things would return to normal.

He couldn't wait.

Or could he?

SHE WOKE TO SUNSHINE and birdsong. Her fever was gone. She was freezing.

Milda kicked off the damp blanket, then grabbed her clothes. Lazlo slept sitting up, his back against the rock. He must have stayed up most of the night to watch over her.

She couldn't forget how he had gently washed her

face and neck over and over again, then carefully wrapped her in the blanket. It was a side of him she hadn't seen before. She had a feeling he hadn't seen it too often in the past, either. She had wanted him so badly to hold her. Had to be the fever, she'd told herself at the time.

His eyes popped open. His dark gaze immediately focused on her. "How are you?"

He looked all mussed and so incredibly handsome that it made her heart ache. *Don't fall for him,* she warned herself, and had a feeling that this would become her new mantra for as long as they were trapped on this island together. "Cold."

He pushed the damp blanket farther away and came to lie next to her, folding her into his arms. As always, he radiated heat. And she found herself molding her body against his. Her muscles relaxed, degree by degree, as she grew more comfortable.

Don't fall for him.

"Stomach pains?"

"None so far. Do you think the worst is over?" Please, please, for love's sake.

"Let's hope. Make sure you keep hydrated." He grabbed a water-filled champagne bottle.

She took it but didn't drink at first. "What will we eat?"

Not that she could think of food at the moment, not yet, but she had to have nourishment eventually. God forbid, Roberto found them and she was washed out and weak. She didn't want to become a liability. She needed to get back up to speed so they could work like a team.

"The food from that pile." He pointed. "I had some of it before, but you passed out."

Caviar galore. She wrinkled her nose. "What about the food we both tasted?"

"I thought about that. But it's possible that there was something that you ate more of than I did. Could be that my level of tolerance for whatever poison was used is higher. We should go with the safest option available. And have more oranges and honey," he added.

Mentioning the honey reminded her of his kiss. She couldn't take her eyes off his face all of a sudden. They were snuggled together in the breathtaking Mediterranean morning, the sea murmuring in the distance, birds singing in the air. She was pressed against him intimately, as if they'd just woken up after a night of lovemaking.

He must have been thinking the same thing, because his eyes darkened with heat. No man had ever looked at her like that before. That look made her feel like the most beautiful woman in the world. He lowered his lips.

To her forehead.

Disappointment sang through her.

But it was for the best. Definitely. One of them had to keep a cool head, and on this morning it seemed that person would be him.

She was grateful.

Under no circumstances would she acknowledge that she was also a little disappointed.

HE FOUND THEM.

Roberto lay among the rocks halfway up the hillside, looking down. He saw some scattered cans and a blanket a hundred meters or so below him. This had to be their hideout.

A difficult spot to approach unseen. They were protected by the boulders. And since Marco hadn't come back last night, he had to assume that they had gotten to him and now had his weapon. He wasn't too upset over Marco. The man had been way too hotheaded. He might have gotten rid of the idiot himself before he left the island. He couldn't afford Marco messing up once they reached the mainland. His big mouth had been the reason they'd been caught and ended up in jail in the first place. And he never did listen.

Roberto had told the dumb bastard not to go out into the night alone. But Marco had wanted the woman badly. Like most young thugs his age, he had little discipline. In any case, looked like he was out of the picture permanently.

Roberto watched his enemies' lair with patience. He couldn't directly approach the crevice. He had to wait for them to leave it, had to be patient until he had a better opportunity. With any luck, they'd go foraging in the woods where he could easily sneak up on them. If they went to the beach—open land—he would just have to wait. Now that he knew where they were hiding, the rest should be easy.

He didn't for a moment consider hiding from them, keeping out of their way.

They'd killed Marco and José.

He had unfinished business with the prince, anyway. And they had seen his face. He was in no rush. He was so close now, the death of those two was a done deal. Everyone back home knew that he never let go of revenge. And he never left witnesses.

Chapter Ten

Lazlo had gone off to find Roberto and get the radio. *To* kill *Roberto and take the radio,* Milda thought. She couldn't picture the man handing over the damn thing any other way. Which meant a fight to the death.

She had refused to keep the gun for that very reason. After some heated words, Lazlo had agreed to take it, but insisted that she should at least have the knife she'd taken when she'd charged in to rescue him.

He was too stubborn to accept that she was too weak to fight off anyone, no matter what weapon he left with her. Her arms trembled too much to hold the heavy handgun steady. Even the knife...

If it came to hand-to-hand combat, she was dead. End of story.

Not that she thought the prince would let things come to that. He would defeat Roberto and then he would come for her. He would get them off the island somehow. She trusted him.

That was new.

So was the bad case of hero worship she was

developing for him. He made sure she was fed, kept her warm and saved her from Marco. And he was a dashing prince. Nobody could blame her if she had a few stars in her eyes when she looked at him.

A considerable change from before they'd gotten stranded on the island.

Desert Island Syndrome?

She didn't think so. She had the opportunity to see the prince under duress, stepping up to the plate, so to speak. And she liked what she'd seen.

Liked it too much, perhaps.

Especially his kisses.

Stop right there. There was no way she was going down *that* road. He was a client. A high-profile client. As high-profile as she was ever going to have for as long as she lived.

Thank God she wasn't developing a crush on him or, God forbid, any feelings. She was definitely smarter than that. The fact that she cared for him was completely normal. She cared for all her clients. A marital consultant was no good without an empathetic personality. And really, there was no such thing as too much caring when it came to another human being.

Soon she would find a match for him and he'd be married to a lucky woman. Very lucky. And the fact that she was feeling morose all of a sudden had nothing to do with jealousy. Which would have been ridiculous… completely.

A small noise came from her right, drawing her attention from the twisted path of her thoughts. She clutched the knife tighter, stiff with fear as Roberto stepped out of the bushes.

Oh, God.

She hadn't killed him then, with that rock. But he would know that she'd tried. She could expect little mercy.

The man pointed a gun at her, identical to the one Lazlo had taken. Standard-issue royal guard weapons. "Toss the knife to me."

He had quick eyes and likely just as quick hands. He probably figured he could handle her with one arm tied behind his back.

He was right.

But she didn't obey. Not the least because her muscles refused all movement.

"The knife." Roberto raised his voice, scowling with impatience. There was something savage in his face, in the way he took a deliberate step forward. His clothing—a Valtrian royal guard uniform he'd gotten from one of the men he'd killed—was dirty and torn. "The knife," he repeated, with venom in his voice.

And she had to admit that she didn't really have a choice. That she could defend herself against a seasoned killer had never been more than a fantasy. She couldn't defeat this man, not on her best day, and today was far from that.

If she put up some desperate fight now, she'd be shot for sure. But if she went along with him, maybe that would give Lazlo enough time to return and save her. She tossed her sole weapon toward the man, worrying that this could be her biggest mistake yet. But the knife was no good against the gun anyway, even if she had the strength to wield it.

He picked it up and stuck it in his belt. "Get up. You're coming with me."

A moment of relief came. Maybe he would take her back to his campsite. And Lazlo would be there, waiting. Then her sad reality hit. "I can't." She didn't have the strength to follow his orders. No way could she march halfway across the island.

"Walk or die." The look in his eyes said it wasn't an idle warning.

I'm walking to Lazlo. The thought gave her enough strength to push to her feet shakily. She took a few steps, steadied herself, took a few steps more and realized she might be able to pull it off after all.

She headed up the hill, but Roberto shoved her in another direction. He wasn't taking her to his camp. They were walking away from Lazlo, not toward him.

She dragged her feet, desperate for an idea that might set her free, trying to come up with something that would help her get away from the man. A quick scan of her surroundings didn't help any. There were plenty of loose rocks, but she was too weak to throw with any force, her arms too unsteady to hit her aim.

"That way." He motioned with the gun. "Keep moving forward."

She did as he asked, hanging her head in defeat, her gaze falling on the colorful beads that circled her wrist. She brought her hands in front of her and slid the bracelet off. He said nothing. She took that to mean he hadn't noticed. So she snapped the band and, every twenty feet or so, she surreptitiously dropped a love bead. The dots of color seemed pitifully small on the ground. Even she could barely see them, and she knew what she was looking for. But she could think of no better way to leave a trail for Lazlo.

Roberto marched her up the hillside, keeping in the cover of the bushes. He kept looking back. Was he afraid of Lazlo? He should be. But thinking of him distracted Milda and she tripped, scraping her palms on the ground. Which was the least of her problems. Roberto swore and kicked her. Pain shot down her thigh. Getting back to her feet took all her strength, but she did it, not wanting to give him any further reason to abuse her.

He took her around the side of the hill, into a long valley she hadn't yet seen. Old ruins littered the hillside here. The view would have been breathtaking under other circumstances.

"That way," he directed her, panting.

She was out of love beads. Desperation made her glance around for another idea, but nothing came to mind. She was too sick and too tired to think. She simply put one foot in front of the other, telling herself that he wasn't going to kill her as soon as they reached their destination. If he wanted to shoot her, he could have done that at Painted Rocks, where he'd found her. He had a plan for her. And if she went along with it, she could gain time, maybe enough time for Lazlo to find them. That was her only hope.

She put one foot in front of the other and plodded forward until he signaled that she could stop at last. She was beyond tired and thirsty.

The large stone boxes and boulders seemed solemn, the figures etched into them barely visible, worn down by rain during the past centuries. Some were broken, some surprisingly whole. One still had its lid on, although shoved to the side.

Roberto picked that one. "Get in there."

She stepped up to it and peeked in, seeing nothing but dirt and leaves the wind had blown inside. Still, the stone box gave her the creeps. "Please don't do this."

His face was as hard as the stone carvings around them. He didn't seem to be in the mood to bargain. He shoved her roughly, banging her hip against the box.

"Okay. Wait." She moved at last. If she didn't climb in there on her own, he certainly had the strength to make her, and possibly injure her in the process.

"Get your head in," he ordered, and swung his arm her way.

She ducked quickly.

"And stay down." He heaved against the lid.

Panic squeezed her chest.

The lid didn't budge. Thank God for small mercies.

"Don't move," he ordered as he walked off.

This was her chance. She had to do something. But she was too weak to take advantage of the opportunity.

If she could climb out and run for the trees… He was coming back all too quickly, with a branch that he wedged against the lid to use for leverage.

And to her horror, the lid began to slide over, inch by inch. Until now, she'd been willing to go along with whatever he said, because she was playing for time. He hadn't shot her immediately. Obviously he was saving her for something. She didn't want to think about what that something might be—using her to trap Lazlo, or worse. But now, as the lid closed above her, she realized that Roberto might just mean to kill her slowly. Maybe he was out of bullets.

She should have thought of that before. He might have been bluffing with the gun. Or maybe not. He'd gotten the knife away from her. If he wanted to kill her, he could have used that, too. She was too scared to think straight, to come up with an idea to trick him somehow, to figure out how to escape.

"Please don't," she begged, the most she was capable of at the moment. "Please. I'll do anything you want me to do. Don't lock me in here." The idea was more than she could bear.

He merely grunted with effort as he worked.

Suddenly, the branch snapped, sending him staggering back. He swore. She looked up through the gap, at the clear blue sky. He might not have sealed the box, but the lid was on far enough so there was no way for her to squeeze out.

He swore again, whacking the lid with the broken end of the branch. She ducked instinctively.

"What happens now?" she asked after he quieted—not really expecting an answer, but unable to stop herself from asking, her heart racing so fast she felt as if she was on the verge of a heart attack.

"You wait for me."

Like she had another choice.

She was alive. She tried to focus on that. It worked for about thirty seconds. Then she thought of something that chilled her to the bone.

What if Lazlo succeeded in killing Roberto, and Roberto never came back for her?

ROBERTO HEADED BACK toward his tent, as satisfied with himself as a man could be. He had a feeling that, when the prince had headed out that morning with a gun, the man was going after him. They were evenly matched now. Each had a weapon. That was why he'd decided to get some leverage.

Now the woman was his, and she was locked up. If things went well and he didn't need her, he could leave her where she was. She wouldn't get in his way again. And he would teach her a lesson, too, for hitting him over the head. He rubbed the bump and winced.

Yes, all in all, she had to die. But if things went badly, first he would use her as a hostage.

José and Marco were dead. Not that their deaths were a complete disadvantage. He might be able to better blend in without them once he reached the mainland. The authorities were looking for three men. Now he'd be alone.

And he had an idea how to reach the mainland. To hell with the raft that could fall apart as easily as the first had. He'd gotten this far. He didn't plan on drowning now.

Eventually, probably soon, someone would come to pick up the prince and the others. There had been four of them on the island. Which meant that probably only one boat would come, two at the most. With only a handful of escorts, if he was lucky.

He could pick them off one by one, as soon as they reached the beach, before they knew what hit them. And then the boat, and freedom, would be his.

WHERE THE HELL was the bastard? Lazlo went through the campsite where he'd been tortured not long ago. A fresh pile of dirt showed him where José was buried. He checked the tent. No weapons. No radio. But he did find the food and water the three men had stolen from his guards. He didn't take anything. If he succeeded in taking out Roberto and getting the radio back, he could call for help and they'd be rescued before the day was out. If he failed…

He wouldn't.

He couldn't let anything happen to Milda. She was the one for him. He didn't stop to examine that thought. He would think about that later. Right now, he needed to focus on doing whatever it took to keep her safe.

As the sun moved higher on the horizon, he headed for the top of the hill to give himself a better view of the island. Waiting at camp would have probably worked,

Roberto would most likely come back to eat. But when? The man could be out there, wandering around the island all day. And Lazlo didn't want to wait. Milda was no longer as deathly sick as she'd been during the night, but he was worried about the poison she'd most likely ingested. He wasn't sure what the long-term effects would be. She needed medical help as fast as he could get it to her.

The sun above was merciless, although dark clouds were gathering on the bottom of the horizon—a storm that might hit before noon, or miss them entirely. Sweat rolled down his face. Low, prickly bushes scratched his legs. He kept going.

The heat was even more unbearable at the top. The faint breeze that moved meant little without any shade. He spotted a couple of fishing boats in the distance, all of them too far away to see him waving. Shooting his gun wasn't an option. Roberto could be close. Lazlo was reluctant to give away his location and have the man sneak up on him. Nor did he want to waste any of his few remaining bullets.

He surveyed the section of the island he could see from where he stood. The beaches and the rocky hillside were clear. Of course, Roberto could be in any of the wild groves. Or on the other side of the island. Taking a look at that required another short climb around the impressive rocks that blocked his way.

He made it over, handhold by handhold, was almost clear when he slipped and banged his bad knee. Sharp stones scraped his skin as he slid. He would definitely be adding new scars to the old ones on this trip. The least of his problems.

He went even slower, and paid closer attention to every foothold. Then he made it to flat ground at last and took a moment to take stock, using his shirt to stanch the bleeding. He didn't mind the pain—he was used to getting banged up on the racecourse—but he wanted to make sure that he was in good fighting shape when he met Roberto, and that meant he had to minimize blood loss as much as possible.

When his wounds were taken care of, he did take a more careful look around. Again, the beach in the distance was deserted. This side of the hill looked over a valley facing another hill that was somewhat lower. Etruscan ruins dotted the landscape here and there. From his childhood visit, he knew there were more among the trees as the elevation got higher. The Etruscans loved building their cities on the top of hills.

No movement anywhere.

He waited at least half an hour, scrutinizing every spot that he could see from his position. Then, when he was nearly ready to give up and try something else, he spotted Roberto, as the man hustled across one of the clearings near the beach.

Lazlo took careful note of the direction in which the man was headed, then took off after him. He aimed to cut him off, but when he reached the spot where he thought Roberto would be by then, he found it empty. Had the man turned? If he hadn't continued in this direction, that meant he'd either turned right, toward the beach, or left, toward his campsite.

Since food and water would be waiting only in the tent, Lazlo headed that way. He moved as fast as he could and as quietly as possible. He meant to end this deadly game of hide-and-seek today. After half an hour or so, he was rewarded by a slight noise up ahead.

He immediately stilled.

The noise was repeated. Someone moved in the woods about a hundred meters ahead, walking away from him.

He followed carefully, lengthening his steps to close the distance. He went around in a half circle, and this time managed to get in front of the man, which gave him the advantage of picking the ground where they would meet. He chose an ancient olive tree for cover. And stepped out in front of Roberto just as the man was plodding through a sparser area in the woods, with nothing to hide behind.

"Put your hands in the air." Lazlo kept his gun on the man.

Roberto didn't even have a chance to draw his weapon. He looked startled, but not particularly rattled. He even allowed a small sneer.

"I want the radio and your weapon."

"And if I don't give them, you shoot me?" The man foolishly mocked him.

"I'd prefer to secure you for now, then give you over to law enforcement later. You don't have to die on this island." He had to give the bastard something to make him cooperate.

But he didn't seem all that excited by the offer. "Better here than in prison." The man spat, his face reddening with anger.

"Toss your weapon and the radio."

Roberto hesitated then shrugged, as if he didn't care, as if he knew the gig was up.

But Lazlo didn't let down his guard. "The weapon first."

As if to spite him, Roberto reached for the radio on his belt instead, unclipped it, tossed it in a high arch. Lazlo could barely see it, having to look toward the sun. He had to move his hands for the catch. He couldn't afford to let the thing drop and smash on the rocks at his feet.

But as he stopped aiming the gun at Roberto, the man went for his own weapon. By the time Lazlo had the radio and the gun trained back on the man, he was facing down the barrel of Roberto's gun.

"There's no need for this. We can both walk off this island," Lazlo said, trying to reason.

"Me walking in chains?" The man shook his head.

"What do you want?" Lazlo pretended that he was willing to negotiate.

"You give back the radio and toss me the gun. And I'll let your girlfriend live."

Lazlo's blood ran cold. Then reason gained the upper hand. Roberto had to be bluffing. The overhang at Painted Rocks protected their shelter. Finding it was nearly impossible unless someone knew exactly where it was.

"She looked pretty sick. You better hurry." The man sneered.

And Lazlo knew that he spoke the truth. He wouldn't know that Milda was sick unless he'd seen her. And if he'd seen her...

The gun jerked in Lazlo's hand before he steadied it. "What have you done to her?"

"LAZLO!" MILDA SCREAMED again, her face pushed up into the gap above her. It wasn't big enough for her to stick her head out and see, but she figured her voice carried better if she shouted straight through the hole. Still, there was no response. She'd been shouting for so long that her voice was hoarse; but she couldn't stop, couldn't give up, even knowing that the surrounding trees trapped the sound, and that he would only hear her if, for some reason, he accidentally came this way.

And they never came to this part of the island. The valley was locked between two hills, without a view of the beach. It was too far from their shelter at Painted Rocks, too far from the creek.

She lay down on the bottom to catch her breath. Her fingertips were bleeding, her arms sore from the effort she'd been putting into moving the stone lid, to no avail.

She was buried alive, in a two-thousand-year-old coffin. And it was definitely some kind of sarcophagus. Enough sunlight filtered through for her to see the images carved along the walls. These were not as eroded by the weather as the ones outside. Faces of ancient gods and funeral processions decorated every inch.

Thank God, the grave robbers who'd long ago stolen anything that might have been valuable had also taken the body. At least she wasn't lying on someone's dry bones. But being locked in still freaked her out in every possible way.

The lid seemed immovable. Even Roberto could only shift it by using a branch for leverage. She had no tool to help her. However, she'd had some time to rest now. And her stomach was no longer as sick as the day before. She felt some of her strength returning.

She certainly had plenty of time to think. What could she use to help herself? There was absolutely nothing in there, save some dry leaves. She was looking straight up through the gap as she racked her brain. She saw storm clouds above and wished it would rain. Then she could push her face in the gap and drink.

Then another thought occurred to her. If they had one of those Mediterranean downpours, could water fill up the sarcophagus? She didn't fancy drowning.

Like she didn't have enough to worry about already.

Adrenaline shot through her, jump-starting her thinking. Maybe she could use her legs. Her leg muscles were much stronger than the ones in her arms. According to a Pilates teacher client of hers, the thigh muscles were one of the strongest in the human body. Milda bent her knees and set the bottom of her feet against the lid, then thought better of it and took off her sandals, thinking that she might be able to get better traction barefoot.

She pushed. Grunted. Nothing. She doubled her efforts until her thigh muscles burned and she felt like her bones were going to snap under the strain. When she thought she couldn't possibly keep up the effort any longer, she pushed harder yet. And then the stone lid moved, even if it was a small fraction of an inch.

Unfortunately, that small movement tilted the corner at the top into the sarcophagus. She caught her breath, desperately trying to support the weight, knowing she didn't stand a chance. But an inch or so below the top, the edge of a carving inside caught the slab.

Not that she could afford a sigh of relief.

That miniscule ledge wasn't going to hold a slab that weighed a ton. Not for long. In fact, she could already see the stone cracking.

And when that chunk broke, the lid would slide lower, tipping in. Sweat rolled down her face, her throat going dry, her heart racing as she realized that all that weight could come down on her at any moment.

"Lazlo!" she screamed, hoping more than ever that he'd be in time to save her.

Chapter Eleven

"Take me to her." Lazlo pointed his gun straight at Roberto's heart.

The thought of Milda being tied up somewhere in the woods, hurting and scared, was unbearable. As many times as he had tried to cajole, threaten or bribe her into going back home in the past five months, now he had a hard time picturing his life without her. Along the way, she had become a constant in his life. He might have even enjoyed their game of trying to outplay each other, their verbal sparring, her wry humor, the way she never gave up, not for a second.

"You will take me to her immediately."

"And if I don't?" Roberto sneered. "You'll never find her without me." Then he repeated his own demands. "Put down your gun and step away from it. *Por favor, señor,*" he mocked.

And after a long moment, Lazlo nodded. He lowered the gun, but then brought it back up again immediately, shooting for Roberto's right wrist. Except that Roberto must have expected some move on Lazlo's part, because the man dove to the side, squeezing off a shot of his own.

But he dove exactly the wrong way.

Lazlo lunged toward the falling body, swept the gun out of Roberto's limp hand. Blood ran out of the man's chest, from the bullet hole that went straight through his heart.

Time stopped as he watched that bright blood running down the man's clothes.

"Where is she?" Lazlo demanded as dark fear rose inside him, fear the likes of which he hadn't known existed. He'd always prided himself on being the cavalier, easygoing prince. Professional racing had been taken from him, so he'd been determined to enjoy what the rest of life could offer. He wasn't the type to get worked up over every little thing. Except Milda had gone from being a minor annoyance in his life to something else. She was important to him. The most important thing he ever stood to lose. The realization was staggering.

So they'd fought in the past. Fought a lot. That didn't mean she wasn't his match in every way. "Where is she?"

Roberto only looked at him with hate in his eyes. He understood that he was dying. He understood it and knew what that meant for Milda. A taunting smile came to his lips.

Lazlo pressed the heel of his hand against the hole in the man's chest. "Don't you dare die, you bloody bastard. You hear me?"

But as Roberto's eyes rolled back and his breathing

ceased with a violent shudder, he knew the man on the ground would never again hear anything. He stepped away from the body, staring for a moment, trying to wrap his mind around what had just happened. Then he sprung into action.

He wiped the blood off his hand, caring little about the smears on his pants leg, grabbed the extra gun and shoved it into his belt along with his own. He put away the knife, too, then took the radio from Roberto and turned the dial as he ran toward the Painted Rocks. When he found the security channel he knew was monitored 24/7, he immediately sent a message.

"This is Phoenix," he said, using his security code name. Each member of the royal family had one. "I need assistance. I repeat. I need assistance immediately. Over." No need to give his location. Royal Security would already have that. He couldn't put it by the Freedom Council that they, too, had somehow found a way to monitor radio transmissions. He didn't want them to know that he was in trouble and arrive before help did.

Barely a second passed before the response came. "Roger that. Assistance is on the way. Hang in there, Phoenix. Over."

"I need search-and-rescue helicopters. Over." He ran down the hillside at full speed, small rocks rolling beneath his feet. He took care not to lose his balance, but no longer needed to worry about making too much noise.

"You got it. Over."

"A full medical team. Over."

"Sending it immediately. Anything else? Over."

"Hurry. Over and out." He clipped the handheld unit onto his belt and kept running, a million things crossing his mind. A million ways she could have been hurt. A million fears that he could be too late.

"Milda!" he shouted every hundred meters or so. But no response came.

He kept himself in good shape, but even so, he was breathing hard by the time he reached their shelter. He'd put everything he had into the mad dash to reach her. But the crevice under the overhang was empty. No sign of struggle, no blood. He looked around carefully. No bullet holes in the rocks. That gave him hope. There was a fair chance that Milda was still alive. But where was she?

He thought of Roberto coming from the valley, and after drinking from their water supplies and grabbing a bottle for Milda, he began running that way. She could be tied to a rock in the punishing heat, for all he knew. He had no idea what kind of shape he was going to find her in.

He kept calling her name, but didn't slow until he reached the valley. Here he made a more careful inspection, called her name more often, waited in silence for long minutes, so that he could hear her answer even if her voice was weak.

Since he hadn't seen her from his vantage point on the top of the hill when he'd spotted Roberto, he guessed that she might be hidden in the woods, so he searched the thick of the forest first.

Nothing.

The thought occurred to him that she might be gagged, which sent a chill down his spine. If she couldn't respond, it might take days to find her on the island, even with a rescue team. And in this heat without a drop of water…

He made radio contact again. "This is Phoenix. I want canine rescue, thermal goggles and night-vision goggles. Over."

"On the rescue chopper already. Over."

"I appreciate it. Over and out." He kept moving, searching the woods. "Milda!" he called out, over and over again.

But no response came and he didn't see any obvious tracks on the ground. Except—

He bent and picked up a reddish bead he'd thought to be a small pebble at first. Then he looked at it more carefully. And up ahead, on the path made by wild animals, he soon found another. A green one. His heart sped. *Milda's love beads.*

Having to look for them slowed him considerably—they were nearly invisible amid the gravel and fallen leaves, but at least he knew he was going in the right direction, bless her brave heart and her always working brain. The fact that the beads were small and hard to see had worked in her favor. Roberto had never noticed her leaving a trail.

He followed the beads for over a mile before he could find no more. Was she here?

"Milda!"

No response came.

He searched every nook and cranny within a few hundred feet. Nothing, nothing, nothing. Could be she simply ran out of beads. The more he thought about it, the more likely that seemed. Her bracelet couldn't last forever.

Still, she could be here somewhere in the valley. Or Roberto had simply brought her this way, toward some other destination. There were a million hiding places on the island. The caves—not that he knew where they were—those Etruscan wells, the scattered ruins.

He'd seen ruins near where he'd spotted Roberto coming out of the valley. But where were those ruins now? The trees around him limited his field of vision considerably. He strode as fast as he could to reach higher ground, so he could figure out where, exactly, that he was in relation to those ruins in the valley.

Twenty minutes passed by the time he reached a high enough spot that wasn't covered by trees, allowing him to see farther than a few hundred meters. Man-made boulders dotted the landscape up ahead, to the east. That was all he needed to know. He was on his way.

The sound of several choppers came from the air before he reached his destination. He didn't even pause. He kept pushing forward. He could see one chopper disappear over the hill, probably touching down on the beach.

He grabbed the radio. "This is Phoenix. Send one rescue team to the valley, to the old ruins. The rest of them should comb the island and keep an eye out for a woman, possibly injured. Over."

"Roger that. Over."

"Thank you. Over and out."

He was at the ruins at last—and realized that he'd made a mistake. The boulders stood in solemn solitude. Nobody was tied to anything here. Any old buildings that might have stood in this place at one point had long ago fallen to the ground, the ruins too demolished by time and weather to hide anyone.

Anger coursed through him for messing up, for wasting precious time. On the heels of that anger came worry all over again. His gut said he was running out of time. She'd been sick to start with, and dehydrated since she couldn't keep anything down. She'd been out here for at least three hours now, in this heat. The climate was much different from mainland Valtria, where it was tempered by the presence of the Alps. Here, in the middle of summer and without any protection, a heat stroke was a serious risk.

He turned to leave, but something slowed him for a second. He saw no hope. "Milda!" he shouted anyway.

The hillside echoed his voice, nearly drowning out the weak response. "I'm here."

Then another frenetic moment came when he couldn't pinpoint where her voice was coming from.

"Where are you?"

"In a sarcophagus." The words came from behind a boulder.

He walked in the direction of her voice and spotted a stone chest. That's when he saw her slim fingers sliding through the crack at the top, and his heart about stopped from the sudden rush of relief. And then he was touching those fingers.

"I'll get you out of there. Don't worry."

Milda yelled, "Wait!" at the exact moment he realized the precarious position of the stone top.

Sweat beaded on his upper lip. From the gouge in the inside carvings, it was obvious that the lid had tipped in at one point and was slowly sliding toward Milda. If he'd gotten here any later, she would have been crushed to death. And that could still happen if he made the wrong move.

"Okay, I see it." He needed to lift that corner before he could do anything else.

"Get a strong branch," she suggested. "For leverage."

One lay by his feet, but it was too short.

"I'll be back." He darted across the uneven ground to the edge of the woods and immediately found a branch that was the right length, but too old and worm-eaten. It easily broke into pieces as he tested it.

"Hurry," came her voice from behind him, too weak for his liking.

"I'm working on it." He grabbed a sapling and heaved, straining his muscles to the tearing point. But he did pull the thing up, roots and all.

He wedged it under the top as soon as he got back to the stone coffin, leaned on the free end with all his weight. The top barely moved a millimeter. The sapling was too young, bending easily.

"I'll help," Milda grunted as scraping sounds came from below.

"Don't hurt yourself." He applied as much power as he could, feeling the veins in his temples bulging.

At last, the top came up a full centimeter. Twenty more and they would be in the clear. "Push again," he instructed.

And Milda did.

A helicopter hovered above, dropping a line some distance away from them. He would have radioed to tell them to bring the line closer so he could tie the stone slab to it, but he couldn't let up pressure now, or the slab would definitely fall on Milda. He kept all his focus on her, fighting for every precious centimeter, barely paying any attention to the men who slid toward the ground from the hovering chopper.

Then the slab was up and supported over the side. He collapsed against the stone coffin, his lungs heaving for air. Milda was panting below. He could only see part of her face. Although the lid was up now, she was still trapped inside.

"Need a hand with that?" Istvan said as he came running. "How the hell did she get in there? What happened here?"

"Careful." He didn't want his brothers rushing in to rescue her, with that wild thirst of adventure that ran deep in the blood of each. And they didn't understand the precarious position Milda was in. "I'll explain later."

"Take it easy." Benedek, his twin, came to stand next to them. "This is a very unstable situation." Assessing that fact only took a glance. He wasn't the best architect in the country for nothing. "Nobody touch anything until I have a look and figure something out."

Janos and Arpad came last. The brothers exchanged glances. For the first time in a long time, the Brotherhood of the Crown, a secret society of some historical significance, was together again.

And Lazlo relaxed a small degree.

One order after another came from Benedek, until he had everyone aligned to his liking. "When I say push, try to push and lift at the same time." He looked at the slab again, running his fingers over it. "I don't think the stone is going to crack, as long as we do this right."

Lazlo drew his lungs full. "We better work this right, then," he added.

Benedek took his place. "Push."

At first nothing happened. Then the stone wobbled. Milda let out a startled yelp. But eventually, between the six of them, the stone lid slid aside at last.

Then he was pushing his brothers out of the way and scooping her out of there. She was sweaty and dirty, her hair wild, her eyes squinting against the harsh morning light. She was the only woman he wanted, the only one he would ever need.

"Are you okay?"

She nodded and buried her face in the crook of his neck. It was a small gesture of trust, but that she would seek comfort from him made his heart soar. This was what he wanted—to hold her and protect her forever.

Istvan brought over the stretcher the chopper had lowered. She looked up, cringed. And Lazlo shook his head. "I'll carry her to the beach." He didn't want to let her out of his arms for a second.

Arpad had a bottle of water for her, and let her drink slowly as Lazlo held her.

Miklos was waving the chopper away, then strode closer. "I'll take her," he offered. "No offense, but you look a mite the worse for wear, brother."

But Lazlo moved forward. Only when she grew even more listless in his arms did he realize his brothers were stronger and could walk faster with her. He agreed to let them take turns.

"The guards?" Janos asked. "Where in hell were they when all of this was happening? Where are they now, for that matter? We tried to reach them over the radio as soon as the report about the boat came in, but they didn't respond."

"We managed to run into a couple of murderous castaways. If you put together a recovery team, I'll lead them to the bodies in a minute."

"What do you mean castaways?" Benedek drew up an eyebrow, as if Lazlo were making all this up.

"From the Sagro Prison break?" Istvan, too, had that look of incredulity in his eyes.

"Sagro Prison?" It was Lazlo's turn for questions.

"Three inmates broke out of Sagro Prison a couple of days ago. There's a massive manhunt going on for them on the mainland," Istvan explained.

Lazlo thought for a few seconds. "Could be them." The circumstances and timing certainly matched.

"How on earth did they get here? Sagro is miles away. They didn't even have a boat from what the news reports are saying."

"They found a way." Then a thought struck him. "How did you get here so fast?" Lazlo asked Arpad, the oldest of his siblings, the crown prince.

"Your boat was found off the Italian coast. A fisherman reported a sunk boat in about twenty feet of water. The Italian authorities contacted us about an hour ago. As soon as they said the name of the boat we got going."

He looked at Milda, but she didn't seem to have heard Arpad's words. Good. She didn't need that burden right now on top of everything else. "I've acted—" He looked down at his feet. "I'm to blame and nobody else."

Arpad opened his mouth, but Istvan lifted a hand to cut off his protest.

Nobody spoke until they reached the beach, except for monosyllabic instructions when they passed Milda over among them, trying to work out what would be optimum for speed. Then they walked out of the last olive grove, and the medical teams descended on the castaways.

Lazlo told them about the possible poisoning so they

knew what to look for, ordering them to give her their full attention, and not allowing anyone to touch him. But Arpad ordered one medic to stay, and there was no arguing with that. He never pulled rank with his brothers as a rule. But now that he had, the medic had to obey. Arpad was the crown prince. He outranked everyone here.

"What happened? You were supposed to come here on a fantasy date." Istvan spoke once Milda was carried out of hearing distance.

Lazlo glared at his brothers, who surrounded him in a ring while the medic worked on him.

"You set me up. Don't think I'm forgiving you for that. What happened to the code of loyalty? What happened to the Brotherhood of the Crown?" Irritation came swiftly. He didn't want them fussing over him like the old ladies of the court, for heaven's sake. He needed to go after Milda and see how she was faring.

Janos drew up an eyebrow. "The plan was for you to spend two weeks on a Mediterranean island with three of the most beautiful women in the country. We didn't think you'd complain."

Lazlo kept up the glare, but glanced toward Milda. Another medic was putting an IV into her arm. "They weren't more beautiful than Milda," he murmured under his breath, without thinking. Then wished he hadn't when he caught his brothers exchanging glances.

"So you noticed her at last?" Miklos bumped him in the shoulder. "Sorry," he said to the medic, who missed with Lazlo's IV.

"No problem, Your Highness. Almost done."

Lazlo kicked some sand toward his brother, the movement making the medic miss again. Not that he would tell them to stay still. The privileges of being a prince. "For your information, I noticed her from the beginning," Lazlo told his brothers, and stilled long enough for the man to get the needle into his arm. He seemed relieved.

"More like took off running every time you noticed her coming," Benedek, his twin, teased.

"I'm sorry I left you two stranded here. I had no idea you wouldn't be safe." Istvan at least had the sense to look pained. He was the most introverted among the brothers. For him, being stuck on the island with a bunch of women would truly have been torture. He loved the ruins, though. He'd conducted several digs here at the beginning of his career. "If I knew you and Milda were in danger… I just thought it would be, you know, romantic." He flashed a remorseful look.

Lazlo shook his head. "Only you would think that a deserted island with a bunch of old ruins is romantic." Then his brain backpedaled. "What do you mean, Milda and I? As far as you knew, I was supposed to be stuck here with the ladies."

"I had some second thoughts about the setup. I called to warn you."

The others scoffed. Miklos said, "Good to know that you could be trusted with a secret."

"I never got a call," Lazlo told him.

"Lady Szilvia answered your phone. She told me

what happened on the island and that they were on the boat, heading back to the mainland," Istvan clarified.

"And the reason why you didn't come to rescue us immediately was what?" Lazlo snapped at him, anger gathering deep inside, when he thought the nightmare of the past couple of days could have been completely avoided.

Istvan's forehead furrowed. "For one, I knew the island was secured. Miklos took care of that. I believed that you were safe. And I was glad for Milda," he added sheepishly.

"What are you talking about?" Lazlo looked around. All five of his brothers looked guilty.

"She would be perfect for you," Benedek put in. "Rayne said so."

Miklos cleared his throat. "Judi keeps telling me the same thing."

"Absolutely not," he snapped, more so because the realization that he was falling for her was still too new to him. He hadn't even shared it with her. He didn't want to share it with his brothers—not yet anyway. He couldn't stand it that his feelings were so transparent. He used to be better at keeping secrets. He'd always pitied men who wore their feelings on their sleeves.

She was smiling at him from a few meters away, as the paramedics poked and prodded her, her amazing eyes shining out of her grimy face. And he felt his heart turn over in his chest and his brain go all mushy. His body went all slack.

"Another one bites the dust," Benedek said next to him with a grin.

"Any guess as to what happened to the boat?" he asked.

"They found a hole in the hull," Arpad said, his voice grim.

Lazlo's limbs grew cold despite the heat.

"Explosives," Miklos added.

He saw red, his hands tightening into fists. "The damn Freedom Council." He got to his feet, despite the protesting medic who was running behind him with the IV bag as he paced. "They poisoned some of the food we brought," he said, then told them that story.

And it was his brothers' turn to look grim. "When you said poison, I thought she ate some poisonous fruit," Janos put in, his face etched in anger.

"So we do have one of their men in the palace. I knew I recognized that voice in the catacombs," Benedek said, looking pensive.

"But now we know it's someone with access to the kitchen. That narrows it down considerably." Miklos scratched his chin. "God help the bastard when I catch him."

The same sentiment sat on all his brothers' faces, and Lazlo suspected on his own as well. His only thought was how to get to the bastard first.

"If we'd known—" Arpad began to say, his tone turning to apologetic.

But Lazlo shook his head. "Never mind that now. It's over. Milda's recovery is the most important thing." But the Freedom Council was going to get its comeuppance. Too many good men and women had died because of them already.

"The gloves are off," Miklos murmured under his breath, then he said as he turned to them, "The second we reach home, I'm beginning a palace-wide investigation. I'll personally interrogate every member of the staff if I have to. The traitor *will* be found."

"I'll be right there to help," Lazlo said, and the murderous looks on his brothers' faces told him they stood ready to do their share to once and for all take care of the rebels.

His attention returned to the women he'd last seen driving off in his boat. "You suppose there's hope for the ladies?"

"Not after this much time. Even if they didn't get hurt in the explosion, there was a storm that night, with strong currents. They would have been washed out to sea." Arpad's voice was as somber as his face. "I'll make sure to personally notify the families. Each was being considered as a possible royal bride."

Lazlo winced.

Arpad clapped him on the shoulder.

Lazlo didn't say anything. The ladies had left the island in a huff because of him. He glanced at Milda, hoping she hadn't heard this last bit of news. She, too, would feel guilty, which was the last thing she needed at the moment. But judging from the tears rolling down her face, she had heard everything.

He took the IV bag from the medic and walked over to her. "Hey, it's not your fault."

Tears filled her dusky blue eyes as she whispered, "Isn't it?"

"Don't think about it now." He gathered her into his arms as much as the medics would allow. "Just rest and heal."

She burrowed against his chest, and it was the most wonderful feeling in the world. Until she said, "You were right. I shouldn't be doing this. I'm going home. I quit."

It was the one thing he'd been asking of her nonstop for the past five months, the words he'd thought would make him deliriously happy. Except, he felt as if his heart was being ripped out. He didn't care a whit about his brothers' knowing glances as he tightened his arms around her.

Chapter Twelve

Milda looked out at the majestic mountains in the distance, feeling small in the endless landscape. She grabbed the carved stone railing and held on tight. So many things overwhelmed her—the mountains; the remote hunting castle where Lazlo had brought her to recover; Lazlo's presence; her guilt over what had happened on the island; the thought that she would be leaving soon and probably never see Lazlo again.

Soft, veil-like clouds gathered above. One looked like a castle. The other… With that curve on the bottom, the other looked very much like her grandmother's face. What would she say if she could see Milda now?

She let go of the stone, blinked hard and turned back toward the double French doors that connected the balcony with her opulent suite. She had to get herself together. She needed to make some decisions. Or rather, she had to follow through on the decisions she'd made during the past two weeks since they'd been rescued off the island, during all those dark nights she couldn't sleep.

Unbidden, her gaze drifted to the right, to Lazlo's suite. And she caught him watching her through his window with that unfathomable look she'd been seeing on his face a lot lately.

He strode outside once he realized that she'd seen him. He was sliding a cell phone into the inner pocket of his jacket. "Miklos sends his regards."

"Any news at the palace?"

"They found traces of explosives around the hole in the boat. Different manufacturers have different markers in their material so it can be traced if those explosives are used in any criminal activity. The charge used to sabotage the boat was made of a faulty batch. If it weren't, it would have exploded much sooner, when I was on the boat. Anyway, only a few hundred kilos were sold before the company realized the mistake and recalled it. Miklos is working on getting the client list."

Which meant that they were likely to find a link to the Freedom Council at last, a link they could follow. Miklos was working the kitchen angle as well, investigating the poisoning. That would be another link. She could tell that Lazlo was excited.

She was happy for him. She could just never be happy *with* him. Too many things stood between them.

"I'm leaving." She was completely recovered from the poisoning—thank God they'd been rationing their food so she hadn't eaten a full portion. Her six-month assignment would be up in another week or so. She had no intention of making any further effort to match the prince, and hadn't once brought up the issue since they'd returned from the island.

A happy client had called her a puzzle master once, someone who had an uncanny ability to recognize pieces that fit together. But Lazlo was a piece that constantly kept changing shape just to spite her.

He was unpredictable, too passionate by half, too easygoing, too focused on the pleasures of life instead of duty—all things that she'd thought she didn't like about him, all things that she'd thought he should change. Except, at some point she'd come to understand that these qualities made him the man he was. The man she'd fallen in love with.

Stupid, stupid, stupid.

"Stay. I'll marry." He vaulted over the railing that separated their balconies. He landed a few short feet from her.

Her heart about stopped.

"Which one?" The three ladies had been found. The Lady Adel had broken both legs in the explosion, but the other two had dragged her to shore. They were all smart enough to wear their life vests, which had saved their lives. The ladies had been recuperating in a small Italian town.

With both of her legs in a cast, the Lady Adel couldn't travel, and the other two decided to stay there with her, out of solidarity. Lazlo had visited them the day before.

She tried not to be jealous. She wasn't succeeding.

He didn't answer her question.

The knife in her heart twisted.

Because the reason for no longer matching the prince wasn't simply her regret over what happened on the island and what happened with the ladies. She couldn't match him because she was in love with him. She'd broken the number-one rule of matchmaking. "I'm leaving," she repeated. "Tonight, if there's a flight."

She hadn't planned on going until tomorrow, but with a royal engagement coming, she felt she couldn't get out of there fast enough. She felt like she couldn't breathe.

"You'd quit on me?" He stepped closer, his stance and face rigid all of a sudden.

"I quit the business. You were right." She drew a slow breath. "When I thought that the ladies were dead, I had plenty of time to think about how I ended up where I was. Truth is, going into the family business was the easiest option I had. I already knew how to do it. My following in her footsteps made my grandmother happy, and I wanted to make her happy. And after she died..." She blinked back a tear.

Lazlo took another step toward her and took her hand.

"After she died, I had no other family. The business became my family. I thought it was who I was born to be." She lifted her gaze to his. "But maybe I'm not. Except that, if I'm not, then who am I?" She'd been struggling with that thought all morning.

"You're who you choose to be," he told her.

She scoffed. "Easy for you to say. You're a prince."

"And you're a vibrant, energetic, honest, intelligent woman."

He was making everything worse. How was she supposed to not fall in love with him even more when he told her things like that?

She stepped back from him. "So you're getting married." She needed to remind herself of that before she threw herself at him and begged for one last kiss.

"Hopefully. There hasn't been a proposal yet."

"The Queen will be happy."

"I'm not doing it for the Queen." He stepped after her. "Stay."

She looked away from him, out at the mountains, not wanting him to see the pain that sat in her eyes. "I can't." She was determined to save herself that torture. She couldn't watch him with someone else. "I'm going home to figure out who I am. Seems like something I should have done ten years ago, but it's never too late. I'm going to have fun trying new things." She could almost smile, as though she believed that.

"You could try being a princess. You never know, maybe it would fit."

A cruel joke to make. She was about to admonish him, but he was going down on half-knee, pulling a velvet box from his pocket that looked shiny with age.

"The thing is," he said, "I already know who you

are. You're the woman I love. And that's all I need to know." He opened the lid, revealing the most amazing pink diamond she'd ever seen, in an ornamental setting that took her breath away. "You don't know what I had to do to get this out of the treasury," he said when he caught her wide-eyed look. "Let me be by your side while you figure out what to do next. Then let's do it together."

Her head was reeling. "This is—I can't. You're a client." He couldn't be serious about this.

"Are we back to that again? Couldn't an exception be made for a prince? I'm used to having exceptions made for me," he added with a sexy grin.

"Why?"

"Because I love you."

Her heart turned over in her chest. She wanted this so badly, she had trouble believing that it was happening.

"The Queen wants a noblewoman for you."

"It's not going to be my mother's wedding, is it?" He brushed that concern aside with ease.

"But what will she think of me? She hired me to—"

"She'll think you accomplished the impossible and she'll be grateful for it. Believe me. Forget the Queen. What do *you* want?" he asked then, turning serious suddenly.

You, she wanted to say, but didn't. Everything seemed so surreal. "It would never work."

"Explain to me why."

"I'm not who you need. You're not who I need."

"Let me decide who I need," he said. "Who do you need?"

She used to be clear on that—she'd filled out the same questionnaire for herself that she had all her clients fill out.

"Let me guess," he said. "You'd like a Lithuanian American, someone who'd help you carry on family traditions. Someone who lives in New York. Someone who respects your business and supports you in it."

"Exactly. The fact that you don't meet any of those criteria can't possibly escape your notice."

"You want the right man."

"What's wrong with that?"

"What about a man who would make your heart sing?"

She couldn't argue with that. Those were her own words, almost exactly. Was he right? Had she been a fool all this time, making the same mistake most of her clients made?

"What about your precious freedom?" she asked. He'd always said that was the most important thing to him.

"If I'm free to love you, that's all the freedom I need."

"And I need an answer that's not quite that glib."

"I realized that loving someone is not a prison. Having your support and companionship wouldn't close any doors on me. It would open up a world of possibilities. I've never talked to anyone like we talked on the island. You made me see things in a different light. You made me understand a lot of things about myself. The truth is, I need you."

All she could do was stare at him.

He searched her gaze. "You don't love me. You still think I'm a no-good rake, is that it? I swear I changed. Let me prove it to you."

"No, it's not that." She knew he had changed. The island had changed both of them. "I do love you. I've been in love with you—but—"

He was on his feet the next second, crushing her to him. "Say it again," he ordered.

She looked up in exasperation and caught sight of that cloud again, the one that looked like her grandmother. She seemed to be smiling.

Her gaze drifted back to the prince. "I love you, but it doesn't mean—"

"Oh, yes, it does." And then he kissed her.

It was different from all the times he'd kissed her on the island. He kissed her like a man kisses a woman he wants to marry. His kiss held endless tenderness and love, desire, promises.

And she believed all of it.

So much so that she got completely lost in him, and the next thing she knew, she was in his arms and he was lowering her to the bed, onto the crumpled sheets she'd not long ago vacated.

"Are we rushing this?" she asked him.

He smiled. "How the tables have turned. If I recall correctly, a few weeks ago you were only too happy to rush me into marriage."

"That was hardly the same."

"I want to make love to you, only you, every day for the rest of my life," he told her.

"It's good to aim high," she teased, dazed by the passion that enveloped them.

He kissed her again, hard, on the lips. "I aim to please."

She had no doubt of that whatsoever. He was peeling her out of her clothes already. Then his hands were on her bare skin, heat and desire swirling through her, making her dizzy.

In another second, he was on the bed next to her, naked.

Wow. Whatever little brainpower she'd still had functioning shut down then—lights out, blinds drawn. She could only feel.

"I love you," he said again as he explored her body with his hands and lips.

"I love you, too," she admitted for the first time without prodding.

And that seemed to be the only permission he needed for thoroughly ravishing her.

"WILL YOU MARRY ME?" he asked much later, with her still sprawled on top of him after their amazing lovemaking, both of them still breathing hard, her body still tingling from the inside out.

"I don't think I should. I should figure out who I am and what I want to do with my life first."

"You mean a new career choice?" He kissed the heart-shaped mole on her neck.

She nodded.

He flipped her so she ended up under him. "Why can't you do that with me?"

"My life is in an upheaval at the moment. It wouldn't be fair to you. You already have everything figured out."

"Hardly," he said. "Except for the part about loving you."

And her heart softened.

"You know," he said as he nibbled her bottom lip, "people quit and start new careers all the time. It doesn't have anything to do with who they're with. We're in love with each other, let's firm that up and get married. Having that sure point will make figuring out the rest of life that much easier."

He was a smooth talker for sure. The more he kissed her, the fewer objections she could come up with.

"It's too sudden," she said in one last-ditch effort, studiously avoiding looking at the ring on the nightstand.

"We've known each other for six months and spent a considerable amount of time together each day," he said.

"Only when you couldn't figure out how to run away from me," she reminded him.

"More fool I. From now on, I'll only run toward you. I promise."

And she could see it all of a sudden, them coming out of some cathedral, rice being thrown and white doves being released. She could hear the wedding bells.

"And if I say no?" she asked, just to be contrary. He'd given her hell when she'd been trying to get him to marry. He couldn't very well expect her to make this easy for him.

"You can't. You make my heart sing."

"If you call me 'wild thing' next, this conversation is over," she joked, referring to the popular song.

"I'm not going to pressure you in any way," he said, apparently missing the joke. There definitely was a cultural gap. But it didn't matter. "I know too well what that's like," he went on. "Believe it or not, some people tried to drag me to the altar, not caring a whit how much I was kicking or how loud I was screaming." He looked at her pointedly. Then dipped his head to her nipple.

Pleasure shot through her. "I refuse to feel guilty for doing my job."

"I never said you should." He attended the other nipple, then moved lower. "All I'm saying is that I'm not going to push you, but I will keep making love to you until you agree to marry me." His tongue outlined her navel.

Heat and need gathered between her legs all

over again. "You can't be serious. We've just— It's impossible."

"People don't say that to royalty." He murmured the words against her lower abdomen. "When a prince wants something, a way is usually found to accomplish it." His hand was caressing her inner thigh, in circular motions, going higher and higher.

She melted into her pillow as she gave herself over to his ministrations. "Oh. Okay. Fine. I'll marry you, for love's sake. Eventually. But I'm not going to rush into anything."

"Why not? Speed is great." He kissed her silly and made love to her all over again.

She felt content. Complete. This was it, this was what she wanted. Everything else would work itself out. She'd found love, true love. For the moment, nothing else mattered. He was right—whatever else she needed to figure out, they would face it together.

Then he asked, "Are you sure you want to quit matchmaking?"

"What? Now you don't want me to?" The man was driving her crazy. "You were the one who got me started thinking about quitting in the first place. You made me question what I want. And I needed that, by the way. So what's this now?"

He kissed her. "Okay. First, I'm who you want, I'm what you need. But beyond that..." He kissed her again. "It couldn't have escaped your notice that I have three brothers who are all confirmed bachelors in their own way," he said with a mischievous grin. "Maybe you could help them?"

She watched him through narrowed eyes. "You want revenge, don't you? For them setting you up on the island."

"I just want them to know the joy of true love. What? What are you laughing at? Honestly!"

And then they sealed the future with a kiss.

* * * * *

Harlequin offers a romance for every mood!
See below for a sneak peek from our
suspense romance line
Silhouette® Romantic Suspense.
Introducing HER HERO IN HIDING by
New York Times *bestselling author Rachel Lee.*

Kay Young returned to woozy consciousness to find that she was lying on a soft sofa beneath a heap of quilts near a cheerfully burning fire. When she tried to move, however, everything hurt, and she groaned.

At once she heard a sound, then a stranger with a hard, harsh face was squatting beside her. "Shh," he said softly. "You're safe here. I promise."

"I have to go," she said weakly, struggling against pain. "He'll find me. He can't find me."

"Easy, lady," he said quietly. "You're hurt. No one's going to find you here."

"He will," she said desperately, terror clutching at her insides. "He always finds me!"

"Easy," he said again. "There's a blizzard outside. No one's getting here tonight, not even the doctor. I know, because I tried."

"Doctor? I don't need a doctor! I've got to get away."

"There's nowhere to go tonight," he said levelly. "And if I thought you could stand, I'd take you to a window and show you."

But even as she tried once more to pull away the quilts, she remembered something else: this man had been gentle when he'd found her beside the road, even when she had kicked and clawed. He hadn't hurt her.

Terror receded just a bit. She looked at him and detected signs of true concern there.

The terror eased another notch and she let her head sag on the pillow. "He always finds me," she whispered.

"Not here. Not tonight. That much I can guarantee."

Will Kay's mysterious rescuer protect her
from her worst fears?
Find out in HER HERO IN HIDING by
New York Times *bestselling author Rachel Lee.*
Available June 2010,
only from Silhouette® Romantic Suspense.

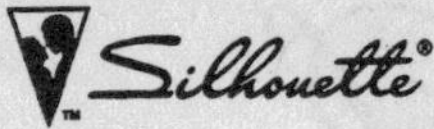

ROMANTIC SUSPENSE

Sparked by Danger, Fueled by Passion.

NEW YORK TIMES AND *USA TODAY*
BESTSELLING AUTHOR

RACHEL LEE

BRINGS YOU AN ALL-NEW
CONARD COUNTY: THE NEXT GENERATION SAGA!

After finding the injured Kay Young on a deserted country road Clint Ardmore learns that she is not only being hunted by a serial killer, but is also three months pregnant. He is determined to protect them—even if it means forgoing the solitude that he has come to appreciate. But will Clint grow fond of having an attractive woman occupy his otherwise empty ranch?

Find out in

Her Hero in Hiding

Available June 2010 wherever books are sold.

Visit Silhouette Books at www.eHarlequin.com

SRS27681